# THE EXTRA

# ANNIE NEUGEBAUER
# THE EXTRA

**SHORTWAVE**

*The Extra* is a work of fiction. The characters, incidents, and dialogue are creations of the author's imagination or are used fictitiously. Any resemblance to actual events or persons, living or dead, is entirely coincidental.

Copyright © 2025 by Annie Neugebauer

All rights reserved. No part of this book may be reproduced in any form or by any electronic or mechanical means, including information storage and retrieval systems, without written permission from the author, except for the use of brief quotations in a book review.

Without in any way limiting the authors' and publisher's exclusive rights under copyright, any use of this publication to "train" generative artificial intelligence (AI) technologies to generate text is expressly prohibited. The author reserves all rights to license use of their work for generative AI training and development of machine learning language models.

Cover and interior design by Alan Lastufka.

First Edition published September 2025.

10 9 8 7 6 5 4 3 2 1

ISBN 978-1-959565-60-4 (Paperback)
ISBN 978-1-959565-61-1 (eBook)

*For Kyle, my plus one.*

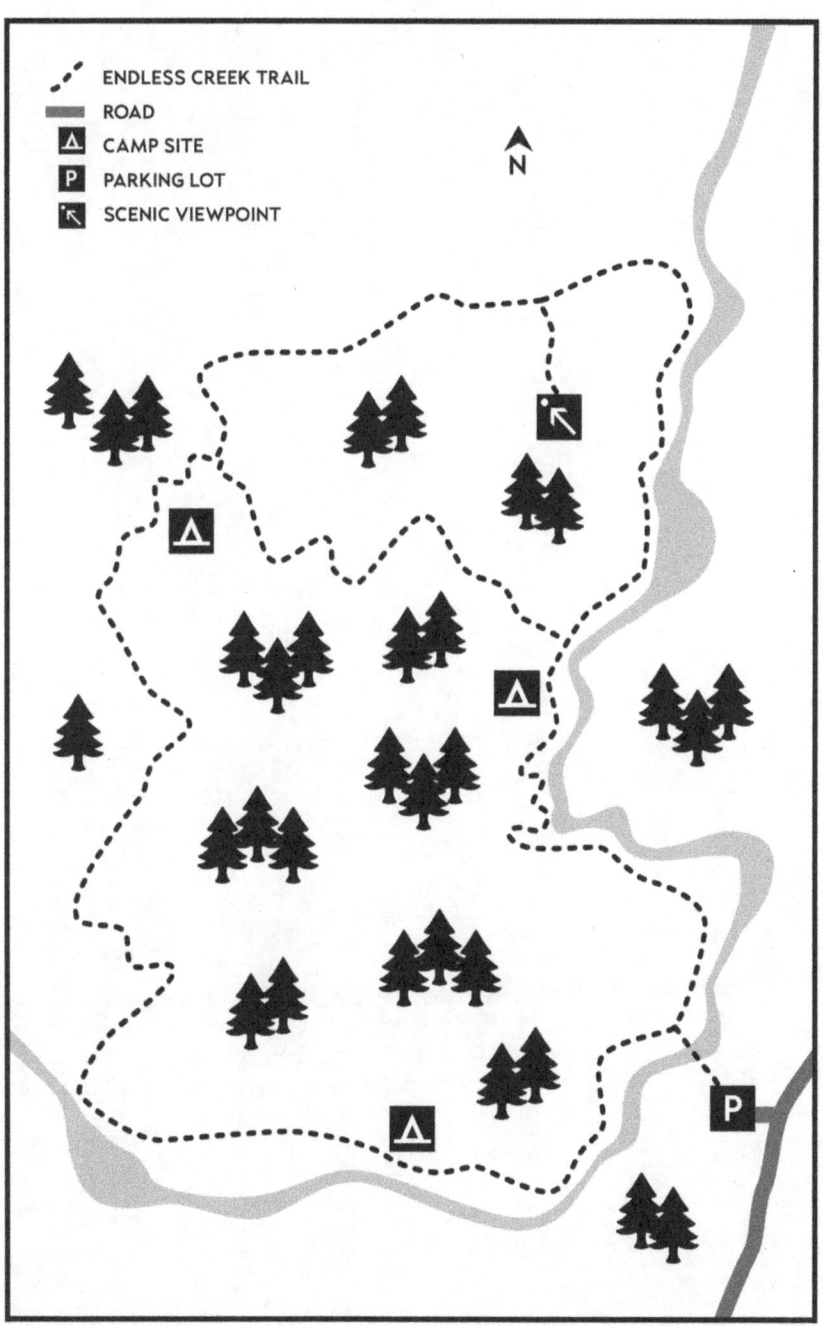

# THE EXTRA

# RULE #1: PLAN AHEAD AND PREPARE

THE EXCITEMENT and chatter of nine warm bodies behind and around me makes it difficult to focus on driving, but I have to—and I have to make it look easy. Somehow as a group they all sense that we're almost to the trailhead, but they don't realize how dicey this section of road is. It's actually two lanes, but this time of year the leaves cover the shoulders and outsides so thoroughly that it might as well be a single lane. I straddle the center line, veering around deep potholes. We crawl uphill at fifteen miles an hour through the darkness, slow enough for my headlights to show me the hazards before I get to them. No matter how many years I've run this trip, this part always makes me nervous. The trailer full of gear we pull behind us adds an extra challenge. Oh, and it's *pouring* rain—so loud it sounds like a single ongoing roar instead of individual drops. Other years the temperature's been anywhere from highs in the 80's to lows below freezing. November in Arkansas.

The turn-off appears ahead, so it looks like this won't be the year I wreck the van. Our tires crunch over the gravel of the small parking lot. No other vehicles are here, which isn't surprising given the shitty weather. In the passenger seat, Bianca, one of the two student trip leaders assisting me, quietly says, "Smooth work, Matt."

I give her a quick nod of thanks before turning to face Joey, my other trip leader, and the seven participants. "All right, everybody. You're going to want all of your rain gear on before you get out." Everyone digging through their stuff and struggling into it while smashed next to their neighbors is a pain in the ass, but cold and wet is not the way to start a trip. It's always amazing the things I have to tell people. They seem obvious to me, but some of these people never even camped in their backyard as kids, much less went on a multi-day backpacking trip. It's never the big stuff that does you in, anyway. It's the little things. A hot spot someone lets become a blister because they're too shy to ask for moleskin. An unbalanced pack. Sunburns.

By the time everyone's out of the van and loaded up, packs adjusted, rain gear in place, van and trailer locked up, I feel as worn down as if the whole trip's already over. I love training the student staff, I really do, but I've been running this trip for too long—since I was a college student myself in the same program. Now I'd rather be home with my wife, warm, dry, and off my feet, but that's the job. The trips go rain or shine, and we're on too tight a schedule to delay. Bianca and Joey, at least, are second- and third-year veterans, so my part should be minimal this time around. Supervisory.

In the dark once the van's lights click off, through the heavy blur of rain, everyone looks the same, like antsy little kids lined up waiting for recess. They face me, Joey, and Bianca as Bianca gives them the 'we're hiking now' intro. Under the shadow of their raincoat hoods, with their headlamps pointing straight out in obscuring beams, their faces are anonymous sources of attention—eyes on me that I can feel but not see. There's always a strangeness to the wilderness at night, especially at first, but it's been a few years since I felt it strongly enough to notice. Bianca finishes with her reminders, and everyone starts moving.

The hike from the parking lot to the first water crossing is less than half a mile, but it always takes longer than it seems like it should. All ten of us have on a headlamp under our raincoat hoods, because it's always full dark by the time we get here from Texas. (We have to leave after the final class of whichever participant has the latest exam scheduled.) Someone always trips. Someone always has to stop and adjust their backpack or retie their boots. Someone is always slower than they should be, despite our pre-trip warnings about fitness level and the strenuousness of the hike—old knee injuries kept secret or a surprise bout of asthma. I'm expecting all of these things.

What I'm not expecting is the shriek one of the women gives out at the front of the line. It prickles my skin, wakes me up. I bring up the rear to keep an eye on everyone, so I can't yet see what's ahead that's scared her. Joey stops, but the rest of us keep moving forward, so the line bunches up. We're at the spot where the tightness of trees opens to the wide expanse of river. I fight not to shove past people to see what's wrong. In the darkness, the water sounds louder than its size, as if we've reached the Mississippi instead of what could probably as accurately be called a creek or stream. Wide, but shallow, and not too fast. Not a big enough deal to shriek over.

I nudge my way through the clustered people to see what's going on. It takes me a few seconds to spot it, because I'm looking for a person or a fallen tree or something dramatic. What my eyes land on, though, is a dog.

He's a mid-sized mutt of some kind, short-haired and long-tailed. His back paws are dipped in the frigid water, as far as he can get from us. Even in the rain and darkness, my headlamp clearly displays the ribs protruding on either side of his indistinctly colored body. Brown, gray, who can tell? His tail is low and limp, ears floppy, and his eyes never stop moving, scanning all of us. He looks exactly like a dog from one of those guilt-you-into-donating commercials. His teeth are bared, but it looks more like a grimace than a snarl, and he isn't making noise. Wary as hell, but he isn't growling or barking, much less attacking. Poor little dude.

I scan the group to see if I can tell who shrieked, but they've morphed into a glob huddled away from the dog. Some people just scream easily, I guess. Being in the woods at night makes a lot of people jumpy, but now my nerves are on edge from the false alarm.

One person is rummaging through their pack, mumbling about giving it food. I say, "No, guys. Don't feed it. We don't know if it's safe."

I look at Joey, reading in his body language that he wants to help the dog. I do too. If someone had found it at the rec center I would've humored them, even helped them look up the right people to call to get it care, but we don't have that option out here. Joey clears his throat, but before he steps forward he asks in a low voice, "You want to hang back to be sure it doesn't follow us, or should I?"

I hesitate. Normally I cross the river first, set down my pack, and come back to the halfway point to help the participants across. But the reason I do that is because I always take the task of the least comfort—or the position of the greatest risk—which is normally being the one to stand in freezing water up to my shins for fifteen minutes. But if the dog were to actually attack someone, it should be me. "I'll take care of the dog."

Joey nods and steps forward to guide the group.

His voice is calm and clear, even through the rain. He tells them all to take off their boots and socks, get out their crossing shoes, and the whole shebang. Even when one of the participants expresses concern over the dog ("We can't just leave him here, can we? He looks hungry."), he firmly guides them away from rallying around saving it. It sucks, but we can't stop a ten-person university trip to drive to the nearest town and look for a vet or shelter. It's after hours anyway. Joey manages to comfort them without lying about what will happen to the animal. I'm proud of him.

Meanwhile, Bianca crosses, drops her pack, and heads back to the center to guide the crossing. Once their attention is all on that, I sort of herd the mutt back toward the trail, the way we came. It twists guilt in me, but I can't see any way around it. I don't have the option of leaving to take him anywhere, but if he tries to tag along it (worse case) puts our participants at risk or (best case) distracts them from the point of the trip. I have to make him leave, for the good of the group. I walk him nearly back to the parking lot, planning to scare him away.

His fur is dripping wet in scraggly rivulets. His tail stays low, but when I look at him it gives the barest hint of a wag.

I can't bear it. I break. Feeling guilty for giving in when I already told myself I couldn't, I grab a protein bar from my pack and open it, crouching to hand it to the mutt. He edges closer, sniffing suspiciously. I'd toss it on the ground but it's muddy. I hold it out so he doesn't have to come too close, and he finally snatches it, jerking back as he wolfs it down.

"Okay," I say, appreciating that he doesn't drop it. "Good boy. That's a good boy. I'm sorry you're stuck out here. I wish I could help." Maybe if he's still here when we leave I can drive by a vet in town and tell him where to come look.

The dog has calmed enough that I decide to give him a gentle pet on his back. Talking calmly so he doesn't startle, I run my hand along his mangy, wet fur. Poor dude must be lonely, because even though he's shaking he lets me stroke him.

I hear something from the trail. When I turn to look, I feel a sharp snap on my hand.

"Hey!" I yelp, jerking it to my chest.

The dog backs away guiltily, his lip coming up in the hint of a snarl.

"You bit me," I say, glancing at my hand. It didn't break the skin. It was not a playful bite, but it doesn't actually hurt. Maybe just my feelings. "God damn it," I mutter. I knew better. My fault, not his.

But this just goes to show why we can't have him tagging along. I make my voice angry and scary. "You go away now. Go on! Get out of here!" I sort of jerk toward him to startle him off. It makes me feel shitty, but it works. He turns and runs to the far side of the lot, and he doesn't follow me back onto the trail. He could probably track us, but he won't want to now.

I sigh, frustrated with myself. That could've been a bad mistake. The rain is lightening up a little, but still a steady nuisance. I remind myself that it could be worse. It could be raining and hot. I get enough heat on the in-state trips. Sweating under a raincoat is not fun.

By the time I make it back to the river, all the participants have crossed and Bianca is on her way to the far bank too. Well, I assume it's Bianca. In the dark, from the back, in their rain gear, everyone looks almost exactly the same—just vaguely humanoid shapes with strange lumps protruding from their bodies. I switch my shoes and wade in as quickly as I can, unused to being the one we're waiting on.

The water coats my feet and ankles in a seamless, breathless moment. Ice cold. The thick soles of my sandals protect my feet from anything sharp, but also make it harder to balance as I walk across the slick rocks. I take my time, placing each step carefully. The last thing I want right now is to eat it in front of the entire group. With my backpack on it would be a fucking nightmare to regain my feet, and of course me and my gear would be soaked for at least the remainder of the night. Not to mention looking like a dork in front of my staff. So, caution.

It's strangely calming. Maybe because I have to focus entirely on moving. For these few minutes, nothing exists but me and the river. When I get halfway, I pause and look up.

The light beams from everyone's headlamps cut through the darkness in random shapes, changing with their movements, shifting angles and intensity based on which direction they face and where they stand or sit to put their hiking shoes back on. The beams look unnaturally white with little moonlight to contrast with, hidden behind clouds. The lights pick out the rain, highlighting its diagonal pattern. I do my automatic count to make sure we're all here. Nine, plus me: ten, all accounted for. It'll make a great picture.

It always takes forever for everyone to dry their feet and get ready to go. I have plenty of time. Still standing in the water, I wrestle the program's waterproof camera from my pack's side pocket and draw it up under my hood to look through the viewer. I almost turn off my own headlamp, but the beam highlights the rain in the foreground while theirs do the background. If it looks half as cool in the photo as it does through my viewer it'll make a great promo shot for the Facebook page. I snap a few, glad I thought of it.

As I'm wrangling the camera into my zippered jacket pocket, I'm charged with a sudden sense of foreboding, like the time I was standing on a soccer field when lightning struck nearby. Something's wrong. I glance at the sky, but there's no sign of the storm worsening, and we haven't heard any thunder. I look behind me, wondering if the dog has followed me back —some type of misplaced subconscious unease—but the bank is empty. I look again to the group, and right as I do, a strange low humming noise hits me. A moment later, all of their lights grow brighter, each headlamp's beam nearly doubling in intensity. A loud, electronic sound fills the air, a sharp, voiceless *ffvvvvvvvvvvvvvt*. The lights shine brilliantly for a few seconds—the source of the noise, maybe. Then they dim, snuffed out. Mine does the same. I hear the surge and death of it directly above my eyes like an electric blow. Blindingly bright; darkness.

The sounds of surprised panic. The girl who shrieked earlier screams again, plus other shouts and exclamations. Someone yells, "Shit!" and then everyone is talking in high-pitched voices. I can't see anything. The surge of light ruined my night vision.

I stand completely still, the water rushing past my ankles. In my blindness, the sounds of the water flowing and the rain spattering on my hood seem doubly loud, intensely close and still somehow distant, like I'm left in a private cocoon of my own personage. I swallow. I can taste the residue of the meal from the diner that stays open late just for us. I reach one hand carefully to press the button on my headlamp, click it several times. It's dead.

"My light is broken," one of the participants' voices carries over the others.

I raise my voice and pitch it so it carries. "Everyone stay put, stay calm. Everything's alright."

Bianca calls out, "You okay, Matt?"

"I'm fine. Y'all good?"

A hesitation, then, "Yeah." Quieter, to the participants, "Everyone okay?" Murmuring from the bank and then Bianca calls to me, "We're okay. All of the headlamps are broken."

*Something is wrong*, I think, and I feel a spike of anger at my disconcerting dread. I'm better than this. I'm the calm one they'll look to for comfort.

My night vision is slowly returning, picking out large, vague shapes like the delineation between the sky and the tops of the forest. The line where the bank meets the shore. Dim, diffused moonlight on the coursing water. My ankles disappearing into it. My own hands, held out to my sides for balance. Finally, the vague, shifting shapes of the people waiting across the river.

What the fuck was that? No lightning struck. Some other sort of electrical charge that zapped our lights? An EMP or something? God, I hope our phones are still working. I'd pull mine out to check it and try the flashlight, but it's tucked into my pack inside a dry bag. If everyone else listened to our instructions, so are theirs —along with any other electronics. I have no idea what we'll do if we can't get the headlamps working, but I do know I'll need to be with my trip leaders and the participants to decide, so I begin picking my way carefully across the second half of the water.

What am I going to do? If I have to guide this group back to the van with no lights it'll take all night. And to cancel the trip once we're already out here? Well, we've never had to do it before. Aside from an evac it's pretty much the worst-case scenario I can think of. Refunds all around, an unhappy director, poor reviews from the participants. By the time my feet meet land I'm already tossing around compromise solutions. Could we camp for a few nights in the parking lot? Some of these folks are so green they'd probably still be thrilled with it.

"Bianca, Joey," I say. I can see figures but not faces.

"Over here," Joey calls from my left. "Sitting on the flat rock."

I pick my way to them, shuck my pack, and sink to a seat beside the smaller figure, which must be Bianca. I've packed my bag carefully enough—and the same for so many times—that I'm able to dry my feet and switch shoes quickly in the dark. Then I pull out my phone, shielding it from the rain with one hand as I turn it on. It still works. No bars, which is the norm out here, but it relieves me. "Everyone's phone okay?" I ask.

The participants all pull out their phones, whether dug from the depths of a drybag and powered on or simply pulled from a pants pocket. The ones that were turned off are okay; the ones that were on are dead. The satellite phone, unfortunately, was on. Joey looks sheepish as he admits that he'd left it on after practicing with it earlier.

I use my phone flashlight to dig out the Ziploc full of extra AA batteries. Even if everyone has either a working phone or a handheld flashlight, we'll need the headlamps. "Let's see if a new battery will do it." I struggle to pop open the little plastic door and swap out the battery. When I thumb the button, the light clicks on.

Everyone cheers, which makes me laugh. I hadn't

realized until now that they'd grown collectively silent as they waited in the dark, like jaded flood victims doubting they'll be saved. The rain has slowed to a gentle patter, too, so the night is almost thickly quiet.

I break it with my voice as I put the working headlamp back on under my hood and reach out a hand for Bianca's. "Now we're talking. Good thing I always bring an extra, huh Joey?"

"You win, boss." He was ribbing on me earlier for being over-prepared. But 'plan ahead and prepare' is literally the first rule in my trip leadership guide, a hodge-podge of outdoor principles, group dynamics, and leadership theory that I train my staff with. Not only did I pack an extra battery for each headlamp, I packed an extra extra, too. Eleven fresh batteries in the bag, and I'm damn glad we have them.

*See? Nothing wrong. Everything is cool.*

Joey rallies the participants as I work. "Okay, everyone. Make sure you've finished drying your feet and changing shoes, then bring your headlamp to Matt so he can replace your battery."

With my own light working it's easier to pop open the casings on the other headlamps. I hand all of the dead batteries to Bianca as I take them out. They look normal, no burn marks or leaking acid or anything. She collects them in a new Ziploc; we pack out all of our trash.

Now the participants are all chattering, abuzz with excitement from the strange phenomenon.

The bag of extra batteries grows lighter and lighter

as the participants move through the little circuit we've set up. When I reach into the bag to grab one for the final participant, it's the last battery. I hold up the bag to be sure my fingertips are right, and it's true. The bag is empty, but I brought an extra. I blink, staring tiredly at the remaining battery in my palm, trying to make sense of it. I know I brought an extra, because Joey joked about it. I'm so certain about it that I actually wonder for a moment if one of the participants handed us their headlamp twice before I realize how goofy that is. I search the ground around the rock we sit on to be sure I didn't drop one. Nope. I must've miscounted—only thought I brought eleven.

It's fine. We have enough. I shrug it off, handing the empty bag to Bianca too while I replace the final battery. I test the light and hand it to the young man waiting for it before hauling on my backpack. One crisis averted, plus a cool story for the campers, not to mention that the rain is slowing down. The sat phone uses a special battery type that we don't have here, but in all my years running this trip, we've never needed it. I think I could get to cell signal fairly quickly if there was a true emergency.

Bianca and Joey are already organizing everyone to start back on the trail toward our first camp. Everyone's excited, talking and laughing with the energy from having survived something startling—like a group of friends leaving a haunted house. There's the tone of a punchline said in a deep voice followed by a sharp peal of laughter and then more jokes shouted over each other's shoulders.

I smile, bringing up the rear. Most of them barely know each other and already they're acting like one big crew, having a blast. I remember now: this is why I do this. Them making memories like this—it's why it's worth it.

# RULE #2: MAKE CAMP ON STABLE SURFACES

SINCE WE ATE dinner on the road, all that's left for this first night is setting up and going to sleep. It isn't until we get into the first camp that I can see everyone well enough to do one of my automatic counts. I try to count as everyone is scattering about, struggling to set up their tents in the damp dark, but they're moving around too much. I start over midway, come up with ten plus me, and start over. I get eleven again. I stifle a sigh. Must be tired.

I take more care, starting at the far left and working to the right. I still come up with ten plus me. I almost say fuck it and go to help Joey with our tent. I mean, I count to make sure we haven't lost anyone. Eight would be cause for alarm, not ten. But if I'm getting ten that means I counted wrong, which means I haven't actually confirmed everyone's here.

I scrub my hands over my face beneath my hood, breathe slowly into my damp palms—mustn't seem annoyed to the participants—and walk to a different spot to get a new view of the area.

I get ten plus me again. It's not a mistake. There are eleven people here right now.

There's an extra.

Underneath my layers, my skin breaks out in chills. From scalp to toes, my body hair rises and creeps. I stand absolutely still, staring, my eyes tracing across the people moving around their tents several more times. Five tents, as expected, but again and again, when I include myself I come up with eleven people.

Who the hell is out here with us?

I begin scanning them more carefully, studying their forms and statures in the cloudy night. My mind is running wild with scenarios and explanations. A stranger who tagged along as we were hiking through. A stranger would stand out in some way. They'd have a different style of pack or gear, or the others would be avoiding them.

I analyze every single figure, but all of them look expected, like they belong. No strange postures, a person standing off to the side, someone not working. It's too dark to see faces from this distance, though, so I begin walking up to each of them under the guise of checking on their progress pitching tents. I try to stay casual, friendly, not wanting to alarm them. I move from tent to tent, touching base, getting close enough to look at each hooded face. I dredge up their names as I speak to them, checking them off my mental list. With each new face I peer into, I expect to be met with the sinister unfamiliarity of a stranger. I brace myself, wondering how I'll handle it when I spot them.

Two of the tents are three-person sized instead of two. That's not too unusual; they're slightly heavier to carry but more spacious. One of them has two male participants who probably just wanted the extra elbow room. The other has two female participants plus Bianca, because we can't put her with me and Matt. We divide up tentmates based on gender and/or friend groups who want to stay together.

By the time I've spoken to everyone, Joey has finished with our tent—and I've accounted for every face I've seen. I know them all. They're all on this trip.

And there are eleven of us.

Could it be a bizarre memory lapse on my part—somehow misremembering how many we have? I know it can't. Not only is it always ten people on this trip, our university van only seats ten people. It isn't possible that we came with eleven this time.

Yet there are eleven of us.

I walk up to Joey, who's zipping a rainfly over his pack in the outer vestibule of the tent. "Hey Joey, will you do a head count?"

He stands, head tilted, but he says only, "Sure boss," and walks out to get a view of everyone.

I set up my sleeping pad and bag inside the tent on autopilot, actually watching Joey.

From the corner of my eye I see him standing still, pausing, then shifting and gesturing to the air in a shadow of a point as he hops from figure to figure for a head count. Another pause, longer. A shift. Sharpened pointing. Something mumbled to himself. By the time I zip the tent and walk up next to him, he's scowling under the beam of his headlamp.

I say, "All accounted for?"

"I—" he huffs, almost a pant from his nose. "I keep getting eleven total. Counting myself. Maybe I counted myself twice."

"Huh. Count yourself last this time?"

He nods, counting aloud under his breath. I'm ten. He's eleven.

"Weird," he draws out, and I can hear the fatigue in his voice. We've all been up since five a.m. to get ready for the trip before work and school, and after the long drive and the slow hike it's one in the morning now. We'll have to wake up in a few hours.

We're standing far enough apart from the group that they can't hear our low talking, wouldn't have noticed our headcount. "Why don't you go check in on each person?"

He turns to me abruptly, eyes so wide they look two-dimensional in the dark. He grips my arm through my raincoat. "You think there's someone out here with us?"

I pat his arm. "I got eleven too. I think I talked to everyone. I just want you to... check my work." How I sound so calm, I have no idea. Inside there's a mantra of *something's wrong, something's wrong, something's wrong,* slinging through my head.

His grip lessens and he draws his hand away,

slowly, like he might want to reach back out. It's a surprising show of fear from a guy like Joey. Not that he's unusually macho, but he's a male college kid, and he's always looked up to me. But my comment seems to reassure him. He nods several times and walks toward the nearest tent, where Bianca and two female participants are rustling around inside the nylon, their headlamps throwing shadows on the fabric walls.

My tension lowers as Joey goes from tent to tent with no outbursts or signs of an interloper. My fear dissipates back into confusion, followed, as he finishes at the final tent, by annoyance. Am I really so tired that I can't figure this out? It doesn't make any fucking sense.

When Joey comes back and echoes my experience earlier—he remembers each participant but there really is one more than there should be—I pull Bianca aside and we go through the whole thing again with her. Bianca is quick, level-headed, and sensitive. She's faster to see the problem, faster to be afraid, and faster to throw out possible explanations. Again, none of them make sense. They're just as stumped as I am.

I pull out my phone, though I'm not exactly sure who I'm going to call, but the cloud cover is too thick to get a signal. If we had a person missing, we'd call off the whole thing right now. But an extra? None of us has any bright ideas.

I gather the whole group together again for a quick announcement before bed. I want them all standing still in one place for a few minutes. They all huddle over themselves now, arms crossed, feet shifting. We're all damp, and, now that we're not hiking, cold. With them lined up, headlamps shining right at me, they look just like they did when we started. Had I counted them then? No, there'd been no need; the van was full, and we hadn't done enough for anyone to wander off.

"Lights off," I say, holding my hand up like they're blinding me. A few chuckles, and all of their headlamps go dark. I let them know when we'll wake up, what to do if they need to go to the bathroom in the middle of the night, etc. As I talk, I look from face to face—shadowed, but more visible than behind a beam of light—counting, forcing myself to draw their names from my memory: Meg and Jo, Pratik, Landilee, Diego, Gary, Brooke, and Rowley. Plus Bianca, Joey, and me. Eleven.

No stranger, no one unaccounted for. Just an extra.

If it's not some stranger infiltrating camp, which is what had me really worried at first, I don't need to stay awake and guard for some psycho slitting someone's throat in their sleep. But still, it's the weirdest feeling. Finally, I chock it up to fatigue and some silly, obvious thing that we just can't see right now. After sending everyone off, I tell my trip leaders to sleep and rest up. In the morning, under the bright light of day, it will all make sense, and we'll know what to do. I think the choice relieves them.

As I lie awake, absolutely exhausted and unable to sleep, the puzzle of it does unnerve me, but it's their relief that worries me most. All three of us are working, but they're student staff. I'm only thirty myself, but they're really still young. I'm the only true-blue adult here, the only professional employee. I can ask for their opinion, but at the end of the day, I'm the one making the decisions.

At the end of the day, I'm responsible for everyone.

All ten of us—or is it eleven?

# RULE #3: GET THE HELL OUT OF BED

THE ONLY GOOD thing about getting into camp so late on that first night of the trip is how cool it is to wake up the first morning. In the dark the participants can't really tell what the land looks like. As we hike in and set up, the colors are all washed away into grays and blacks beyond the beams of their headlamps. They're focused on things like not tripping during the water crossing and whether their shoelaces are too tight. They keep their heads down all night, especially in the rain we've had this year, and go to bed in a tent.

When they wake up and step out, it will feel like being transported into the middle of a postcard. Arkansas in November is almost unrealistically beautiful, especially to Texans who rarely see such colors in nature. The forest all around is a riot of orange, gold, crimson, yellow, and rust. So vibrant they seem almost braggy. I've been on this exact trip over ten times now, and when I step out again this morning, I'm counting on it to steal my breath away as it always does. For the trip leaders and me it's a more gradual reveal—we wake before full light, no snooze button when you're running things—but it's still breathtaking.

The rain has gone, and the air is sharp and cold. Heavy clouds are still covering the sky, but even in that shade and pre-morning dawn, the colors are like a slap in the face. As always, I'm the first up. I stand, still and silent, waiting to feel refreshed, awed, belonging—any of those things that made me first fall in love with this—the reason I care to introduce others to it.

I feel awe, but it's tinged with a bad feeling. Nerves, doubt. That same echo: *something's wrong*. I didn't sleep. I didn't wake up with the answer seeming obvious. I don't suddenly know what to do.

A few minutes later, Joey and Bianca climb softly from their tents and join me where I'm boiling water for coffee on a camp stove. We huddle around it, silent until I finally ask, "Any bright ideas?"

They both shake their heads. Joey says, "Maybe we've always had eleven and we're all just trippin'."

I'd wondered the same thing last night. "The van only seats ten. Don't you think we'd remember if someone sat in someone else's lap?"

Bianca sucks in a fortifying breath. "I want to count again."

"We all counted several times."

"Yeah but now it's morning," she says, as if her meaning should be obvious. When I only stare blankly, she adds, "Maybe they left."

"The participants?" I ask, alarmed.

"The extra one. Maybe that one just went away and now there'll be ten again."

Jesus Christ, I don't know what'd be worse: still having an extra or having lost one. And how would we know that the right one is gone now? My stomach knots and loops on itself. I don't want to be here. I flat out don't want to be here. "That... would not be a good thing," I drawl.

Bianca's face pinches into the center, like she's about to burst into tears.

I rush on, hoping if I keep talking it'll distract her. I'm not the best with people crying, and the participants will start waking up soon. Not encouraging to see their guides in tears. "Did either of y'all count earlier in the trip? Before we got into camp?" They both hesitate. Do they think they'll be in trouble if they forgot to check? I add, "It's okay if you forgot. We need to know."

Bianca's voice is low. "I didn't forget. I got ten right before we crossed the river."

Joey confirms: "Ten at the trailhead, fresh out of the van."

My little bout of pride that they both remembered to count unprompted by me is doused by their confirmations. Still, I say, "Maybe the damn van seats eleven. Maybe we just always called it a ten-seater and never bothered to count?"

They both stare at me miserably.

The first participant is coming out of one of the

tents, noisy and graceless. I say softly to Joey, "Get out eight of the breakfast bars. See if there's one left after everyone else gets one."

Bianca asks, "What are you going to do?"

"I'm going to go count the seats in the van." I say it with enough exasperation that neither of them needs to point out how senseless that is. That or they're both scared enough that they want me to do it too. It's the only remaining explanation that makes any sense to me. "Stay here, watch everyone. Count, but try to act normal. Don't worry them. Keep your heads on, and I'll be back before you've packed up camp."

With each instruction, they seem to be visibly pulling themselves together. Their spines straightening, shoulders settling, chins lifting. They know their jobs, and they're doing their best to live up to my expectations. This time the pride does outshine my worry. They're growing right before my eyes. This is why I love this job. Not the nights on the hard ground or the whiny participants or even the repetitive trips to places that used to thrill me. No, it's these college kids. It's leading them.

I give them each a fist to bump, which sneaks smiles out of both of them—pretending to roll their eyes at how old and uncool I am, but secretly pleased by the attention.

With that, I grab the brain of my pack—the little detachable top part that holds the essentials—and sling it crosswise over my shoulder. I want to get out of camp before the participants notice me leaving or think to ask where I'm going. I could wait to see if there are somehow seven now, instead of eight, but there won't be. I just know, in the same, deep, persistent way that I know that something's wrong.

In minutes, I'm striding down the trail the way we came.

# RULE #4: STAY ON THE TRAIL

**THE HIKE IS JUST LONG ENOUGH** for me to stop turning the puzzle over in my head for a few moments and actually enjoy the view. The woods are bare in the center, trunks exposed, then full in the treetops. The leaves that remain are brilliant, autumnal in the growing daylight. The bases of the trunks have a layer of dry, brownish gray leaf fall that died first. This year our trip fell on the far side of fall; no green remains.

Which is why the vivid green ahead catches my eye. I glimpse it through the tree trunks a couple of bends away. My gaze fixes on it and my pace falters, then speeds up as I round the curves in the trail to see what it could be. The tint is so bright it's almost unnatural, a green bordering on neon, like the freshest shoots of spring. At first I think it's a dropped piece of gear, that safety green common on backpacks and shell layers, but as I near I can tell it's too large. The river rushes nearby, the sound larger than the reality.

Finally, I stop, looking down. At my feet there's a large patch of effervescent green grass, plush and springy like sports turf or the lawn of a castle garden. Utterly out of place.

I actually say aloud, "What the hell?" just because it feels like someone should be here with me to see this. It's too fucking weird. I fish out my waterproof camera and snap a shot of it to show my wife when I get home.

I'm not sure why, but I don't want to step on it. I walk around it, having to edge far enough to the side of the trail that my back scrapes along the brush. It's about six feet across, circular, taking up the majority of the space between the riverbank and the place where the woods close back in to form the trail to camp. It's strangely plush, the blades fine and close together, although there are some patchy streaks where the muddy ground shows through. We must've walked right over it last night. I fight the urge to look behind me, then do it anyway.

Still not having a good reason, I avoid stepping on that grassy expanse as I switch to my sandals and tie my boots around my pack strap to wade across the stream. It's a pain in the ass, yes, but at least now I can see, and I don't have my big backpack on. The water closes in a familiar icy swirl over my feet and ankles, sliding up to my mid-shins like cold silk as I get to the deepest parts. Then I'm across, walking quickly down the trail. If I were with anyone else I'd stop to dry my feet and put my hiking boots back on, but alone I decide to move fast and power through it. I'm eager to count the damn seats and get back to my trip leaders.

Alone, in the daylight—though still dim and gray in the heavy cloud cover—I move fast. In minutes I make it back to the parking lot, where our van remains the only vehicle. It has the tiny little luggage trailer behind it, the side of the sliding door branded with our university program logo. All is still, empty, and I realize I half-expected different, as if by coming back early I might catch it by surprise.

I pull out my key and open the passenger side door, climbing in and shutting it behind me. I take a moment to lean my head back, eyes closed on a huge sigh, then turn to count the seats.

Driver and passenger up front, me and Bianca. A tight row of three right behind us that had Joey and... who? Pratik, maybe? And Diego? Or Landilee? I don't know; it doesn't matter to me where people sit, so I don't notice it. A truncated row of two behind that, to one side so there's space for people to get in and out. And another full row of three in the back. I count several times, starting in different places, but it wasn't a stupid mistake. There really are ten seats. I wasn't wrong or forgetful or nuts. There's no other possibility.

We have an extra person.

Then how do I remember everyone?

The answer comes to me unbidden, as if in a

spoken voice, though it's only in my head: *You don't actually. You only think you do.*

I only think I do? That doesn't make any sense. I have memories of each person; I'm certain. If I'm wrong, it could only mean that the memories of one of those must be false.

I stare vacantly at the empty seats, slightly warmer in the familiar van than out in the wind, trying to process what I'm thinking, feeling. A fake memory? But how? How could Joey and Bianca have them too?

I don't bother trying to tell myself my skin is clammy from my cold, bare feet. I am creeped way the fuck out. I pull out my cell phone and turn it off airplane mode just to check, but of course I get no signal out here. I even, for a few moments, consider taking the van and driving away. *Get the fuck out*, that voice hollers in the back of my head, but even as I think it, I know I won't do it. I won't abandon my trip leaders here—not even for a few hours to go and come back—not when their cell phones don't work either.

Panic threatens to take my composure. I turn to face forward, hands on my knees. They drum a nervous tattoo, but I force them to stop.

I can't leave. I can't call. And I can't trust my memories of the eight participants, because one of them is...

*Planted.*

I ignore that voice.

One of them isn't true.

Okay, so I'll head back and catch up with the group

before they start today's portion of the hike. It's a long, full day, and if we're going to cancel the trip or stay put, we need to decide before everyone starts moving.

I take three deep, slow breaths and get out of the van, locking it behind me as I hurry back the way I came. I could be losing my mind, but I don't feel like I am—and what's the likelihood that Bianca and Joey are also losing theirs in the exact same way at the exact same time?

I'm about halfway back to the water crossing when I remember the photos I took last night, right after everyone had crossed. I stop so abruptly that if anyone'd been following me they'd have slammed into my back. I pull the camera back out.

It was raining, dark. Right before all our headlamps went out. I hadn't bothered checking the picture. I turn it on and click the folder, flipping back one to find the final shot from last night. I pull the screen close to my face.

I'd been right to seize the moment. It's a seriously cool picture. My headlamp cuts a broad, angled swatch across the nearest darkness, leaving only the bottom corners in pure black, petering out partway through, highlighting the rain in almost comic-book-like definition. Beyond that, multiple light beams carve geometric shapes across the distant darkness, highlighting random objects in odd relief. A backpack, a boulder, a tree trunk, the sky, the ground.

It was right before the surge and outage. Was everyone there then? I count them. Nine, plus me.

Relief and disappointment both battle with confusion. I lower the camera, looking up at the clouded sky while I think. No extra.

Of course, maybe one of them just didn't have their light turned on.

I snap my head back down, looking again, this time for a figure not lit by their own beam.

At first, I think I've spotted them almost immediately. Right in the center of everyone, standing straight, a tall, darker shadow in the darkness, untouched by the lights. An eleventh.

Then counter-thoughts crop up. Why *wouldn't* they have their light on? Why would they be just standing there, straight up and down and seemingly unmoving? I get the vague impression that they're facing me, the camera, and simply staring at me with arms down by their sides. Eerily poised. I get chills, then scowl, trying to dissipate them.

It's just a trick of the camera. A specific fall of shadows, of rain, of distance and blur. It happens all the time. Photos that look like one thing but are actually another. Unfortunate angles that make arms disappear, faces double, eyes glow red.

Now that I've thought it, I realize the figure isn't quite right to be a participant anyway. No person is that tall. To be where it looks on the screen, they'd have to be standing right in the thick of everyone, but they're a foot or two above even the tallest person. Plus, they're too narrow, even if in profile. Not enough definition for limbs and no bumps for gear. Too uniformly dark—no variation in shades like where a raincoat meets wind pants. It's just a shadow. Just a long, thin, unfortunately shaped void that first looked like a person.

Just to be sure, I flip back through the other shots I snapped in rapid succession, but there's no variance. Whatever trick of shadow it may be, it's in every shot. I study the other areas of the images, but there are no extra people. Just the nine under their headlamps, putting back on their boots as I stood halfway across the river, taking their picture. Ten of us.

Fumbling to put the camera back into my pocket, I keep heading toward the river. My feet are freezing, shoulders tight, fists clenched. I honestly don't know what to do. I round the bend that brings the river into view and stop again.

From this angle, I can see the patch of green on the opposite bank much more clearly. Distance and the gentle upslope of the bank closest to camp put it in ideal view. I'd thought of it as circular, but that didn't cover it. It's a nearly perfect circle. Pristinely round.

And the random patchy streaks aren't random at all. They're clean, geometric. Patterned. They make me think of pyramids and ancient symbols. But then I picture it less from the angle I have and more from a bird's eye view, and the patches look like places where that unnatural grass has been forced back into the earth. Like some large stamp came from the sky.

My already-present goosebumps come alive as if they're trying to crawl off my body. Against my will, I look up. The sky is covered so fully by the gray clouds that it could've been wiped out and I wouldn't know. Colorless. Drained. Maybe the blue is gone forever. But the green...

*Crop circle.* It's the phrase I've been hedging around. It floats to the top of my mind so swiftly I almost say it aloud, just to release it, but I don't. I clamp my jaw against it, my teeth chattering. I'm way too cold. It was stupid not to dry my feet after crossing, but I was in such a rush trying to get back to my staff, the participants. It's not a crop circle. Those are huge, pressed in dead grain, tamping down a pattern. This is almost the opposite. A small burst of life brought into place where there shouldn't be, growing a pattern. There's not grass on this side of the river closest to the parking lot, or anywhere else along the bank as far as I can see.

It's only there, right where the group was last night when I took the picture.

That strange, shadowy illusion. The dark shape, still and thin and too tall.

The extra.

I have to get back to the group, to Joey and Bianca. There are seven participants that we're supposed to guide, to protect. It's not just our job; it's our responsibility. Our duty. They trust us to keep them safe when we bring them out here. Just as my trip leaders trust me to keep *them* safe.

My fingers are frozen, clutching the camera where it's half-jammed into my pocket. I yank it out and take a picture of that green from this distance, so I can see the whole thing. Then I shove the camera back, zip it in, and cross the river so quickly it's a fucking miracle I don't bust my ass, but somehow I make it to the far shore upright and mostly dry. I want to run full speed to the camp, but I know it's too reckless. I'm constantly lecturing my student staff that self-care is the first step to caring for participants. I edge around the circle of green, not touching it. I really don't want to touch it. I throw a nearby rock into the center of it. Nothing happens. I force myself to stop and put on dry shoes. Then I'm back up and barreling down the path, no longer able to contain my need to run. The trees blur by in great streaks of warm color, as they should. As everything out here should look. Autumn, not spring.

I leave that patch of outlandish green behind, but I know now with primal certainty that I'm running toward its maker.

# RULE #5: LEAVE ONLY FOOTPRINTS, TAKE ONLY PICTURES

THE FIRST SOUNDS from camp slow me. The first voice stops me in my tracks. I stand, panting, on the leaf-covered trail, so out of breath from my speed that I bend over, hands on knees. The voices are calm, cheerful. The sounds of participants in awe as they embrace their first day in the wilderness. The trip leaders encouraging people to eat more. Morning sounds. Everything is fine.

It's enough to make me stay longer, thinking. I pull water from my small bag and drink half of it down, the coldness good in my burning throat. Everything's fine? I'm not sure what I expected, but it wasn't this. Normalcy. Maybe I pictured screams, chaos, fear. I guess I thought they should feel how I feel—that there being an eleventh here is deeply, electrifyingly wrong. But of course, they don't know yet. Not the participants, anyway. Even my trip leaders don't know yet what I know: the confirmation of ten in the van, the circle of green, the figure in the picture.

I can't go running into camp terrified. I'll scare everyone and cause a panic. The last thing we need are terrified participants. Not to mention letting the. . . extra know that we're onto them. What will they do if they know we've realized? What do they want? Why come here, pretend to be one of us? Intruder, infiltrator, faker: words bubble up rapid fire, and I try to tamp them down. I can't panic either. I can't show weakness.

The thought of it makes me queasy with dread. I've never felt so uncertain out here before—so out of control. I can't let the extra see how shaken I am. Or the participants. Or even my trip leaders. Joey and Bianca need to know what's going on, but they also need me to stay level-headed. I can do it for them. I have to.

I take one more swig of cold, crisp water, cap my bottle, and put it back in my bag. I stand up straight, adjust the strap across my chest, and walk calmly into camp.

Bianca is packing up the kitchen. She hands me a breakfast bar and an apple, and I can tell by her sad look what she'll say. "There weren't any extra bars. We handed out all eight."

I knew they would. "Alright." I think for a moment, shoving the bar into my pocket and taking a huge bite of the apple. It tastes like a sweet ice cube. I don't want it, but eating it is easier than putting it away, and, again, I know I have to take care of myself. Skipping breakfast won't keep me at my best. So I crunch through it as fast as I can, huge bites, the cold of it making my teeth ache as I come up with a way to pull my trip leaders aside.

I walk to the center of the camp, mostly packed up now, though a few people still struggle with bagging their tents. I can't resist doing a quick count to confirm there's still an extra, which there is. "Alright, everyone," I call. They all look up, pausing. "You have twenty minutes to finish packing, finish breakfast, use the restroom, and do a full gear check. Everybody good for a bit?"

I look at them all as they nod and murmur their assent. I look from figure to figure, individual, poking at my memory of their names, but they are all still here, all the same, all familiar. Rowley, Gary, Meg, Jo, Landilee, Pratik, Diego, and Brooke. Looking into their eyes one by one makes me clench my fists in my pockets. Shaking my head, I say, "Good deal. Get at it."

Then I pull Bianca and Joey aside, leading them far enough up the trail that we can't be overheard. I show them the photo of the green circle. Then the one I took last night. "See anything?"

They both lean over the camera, Bianca hugging herself tight, Joey with his hands shoved deep in his pockets. I wonder if his fists are clenched too. Bianca says, "I only see nine, plus you."

"Lights," I say.

She glances up, her face close enough to mine

where the three of us huddle together that I can see how chapped her lips are, the white gunk that lines the middles of them. She frowns, a question.

"You see ten lights," I clarify.

Her eyebrows jump, then she bends again to look closer. It's Joey who sucks in a quick breath. "There's another." He points at the shadow.

Bianca takes a step back, a large one. She mutters something that sounds like, "You've got to be," as she walks in a tiny circle in-place. Then she steps back to stare at the small screen. "It's too tall. And skinny. Matt," she says, and it's a plea bordering on a whine. "Matt, no."

Joey has taken the camera into his own hands, flipping through the different shots. The several in a row that all show the shadow, then the circle. He says, "Well we can't go home."

It makes Bianca gasp.

Joey adds, for her, I think, "Not yet."

I ask, "Why? We could find a way to cancel the trip. Make up a reason."

He looks at me, and I'm reminded that I tend to underestimate him. He doesn't talk smart, but there's a type of intelligence there that's easy to overlook. "Because we can't take it home with us," he says. "Whoever—whatever it is, we can't bring them back to the rec. We can't come home with an extra."

"Oh my God," Bianca says, voice wet with emotion. "Oh my God. We only have ten seats in the van. Did you check?"

I nod. "We weren't wrong. There's ten."

"Well then what are we gonna do?" Bianca asks.

I say, "I guess we have to figure out which one it is."

Bianca asks, "How?"

"I have no idea," I admit. "But what else can we do?"

They both stare at me with wide, wide eyes. Joey whispers, "And then what?"

I shrug, fear making the motion too harsh. "And then make sure that one doesn't come back with us."

"Leave them here?" Bianca says, voice lowered into a hiss. "You've got to be kidding, Matt. We can't leave behind a participant."

"Not a participant," I correct. "The extra—the other one."

Joey says, "But how will we know?"

"It doesn't matter," Bianca interrupts, "because we are not leaving someone behind. No way."

"Bianca," I say, "We don't have any other choice. Even if it was a good idea to bring them home with us, there are only ten seats in the van."

"I wonder if everyone remembers where they sat?" Joey ventures. "We could ask them all and compare their answers?"

"How would we explain that?" Bianca asks.

I squint, trying to picture it. "Even if they weren't weirded out by a pop quiz on their seating, if the extra can make an entire false memory for all of us, I'm sure it can make a memory of a seat in the van too, right?" I feel almost nauseated by the thought of not being able to trust my own memory. Shaking my head, I reiterate, "We can't bring it home."

"They could sit on someone's lap. Squeeze in. Ride in the freaking trailer!" Her voice is rising enough to make me cringe. I don't want the group to hear sounds of arguing.

"We can't bring that thing back with us," Joey says gently. "It's wrong. Can't you feel it? Whatever it is, it's bad."

I nod. It's what I've been feeling this whole time. Something is wrong.

"No," Bianca says, crossing her arms. "I don't feel it. I don't feel anything except confused. There's an answer to this. We're just letting our imaginations run away with us. We'll figure it out. We don't need to jump to extremes."

Her stubbornness makes me think she's lying—even if just to herself. She has to feel it. She's as unnerved as we are, but she doesn't want to face it. I get that. I wish I didn't have to either. I can let her hang on to that, for now.

"That's true. No need to make a decision yet. We'll just watch and talk to everyone and I'm sure we'll figure out who it is—what's going on." I hope I sound more confident than I feel. How the hell will we figure it out?

Joey surprises me by pushing harder. "We can't take it home."

He's right. Not only logistically. It's more than

that. It's like a type of. . . loyalty, or something. Or something even more basic. Safety, maybe. Whatever the extra is, it's not good. It's not one of us. And we can't just pretend it is and take it back home.

"Do you really want to?" I ask Bianca.

She hesitates, then shakes her head. "I guess not." So she does feel it, that it's wrong. Somehow that makes me feel better—to at least know that both of them sense it as strongly as I do. "But I don't want to leave someone here, either," she adds.

Joey shakes his head but says, "So what then? Keep on keeping on?"

Bianca says, "We could stay at this camp. Even if we can't go home yet," her voice cracks over *yet*, "we could at least not start on the rest of the hike. We could at least stay close to the van."

I shake my head. "If we don't go on as planned, it—they'll know we're onto it."

"It might know anyway," Joey points out.

Bianca's eyes are glassy with fear.

"Maybe," I agree. "But even if it knows, the participants don't seem to. We should keep them calm and happy as long as possible. This could turn into panic city—or a witch hunt—real quick. Let's pretend everything is normal until we can figure it out."

We have to go on as planned.

As if echoing my thought, Joey says, "We have to follow the plan. Continue on."

Bianca makes no sound, but tears slide down her cheeks as she nods.

# RULE #6: ASSUME EVERYBODY LIES

IT'S the first of two full hiking days, not counting last night when we hiked in, or the final morning when we'll make it back to the van—when hopefully ten of us will make it safely back to the van. Who the hell is the eleventh?

I always hike in the back so I can keep an eye on everyone, and my eye is always sharp because it's my job to pick up on things before they become problems, but now I'm watching the ten people in front of me in a different way than ever before. Usually, I'm looking for potential personality conflicts, troublemakers, and logistical problems. Now I'm studying the people, trying to find which one could be taller, thinner, shadowier than they seem. Which one doesn't belong.

Joey and Bianca trade off who leads and who takes the middle. At the moment, Bianca is up front—almost. Rowley is ahead of her, hiking fast to show off. Often there's one of his type on a trip: a young, fit, attractive guy who flirts with the prettiest girl. Rowley is a music major; I remember him carrying his huge cello case to a pre-trip meeting. He's tall enough that our large backpacks look small on his shoulders. He's already offered to carry Meg's pack for her.

Luckily for us, because we need everyone to carry their own weight, Meg said no thanks and started giggling with her friend Jo, a short, androgynous, non-binary student who Meg introduced as her "bestie" at the pre-trip meeting. Rowley shrugged and walked twice as fast as if to make up for too light a pack. Bianca is not quite authoritative enough to make Rowley walk behind her. Or maybe she just doesn't care, knowing he'll have to keep coming back and waiting for her every time he reaches a questionable turn in the trail. Already I'm a little tired of Rowley. It's not the show-off thing—I was a college kid once too—it's that he keeps making fun of Pratik's selfie stick.

Pratik is a foreign exchange student from India, probably early twenties. He too is toward the front, but respectfully behind Bianca, excitedly taking pictures every ten feet or so. He brought four backup batteries for his phone camera. He's our most challenging eater on this trip, just picky, though non-binary Jo was a close second with their vegan diet. I go through these things as I watch them interact, checking my memory of each for holes or soft spots. Who doesn't belong? How can my own memories be false? How much else of what I think is true is falsified, tampered with? I shake my head. That's a thought spiral that does no good. Focus.

Jo and Meg, the one Rowley's showing off for, hover in the middle of the group, chatting with Joey. Meg is the pretty one. I think of her that way not because I care that she's pretty, but because the prettiest one in the group often sets a certain tone for the rest. Meg is the type who brought shampoo. She's afraid of bugs. She's nice, friendly to the other participants, but sticks to Jo's side like glue. Of the pretty girls, we've had far worse. I once had someone bring a hair dryer.

Jo is quiet, but smiley. They wear a beanie that covers their hair, though dark side-swept bangs stick out in a way that looks intentional. They don't talk much, but I remember Jo speaking up during the pre-trip meeting to share that their preferred pronouns are they/them. They seem to want to make everyone else on the trip laugh—especially Meg—and are quietly good at it.

Walking at the very back, hovering around me, is Gary. Gary is by far the most annoying. Ironically, Gary is what in my head I call "the Larry," which is the guy who just doesn't get it. Gary the Larry is easy to remember not just because of the moniker—memory tricks are great when I'm learning seven—eight—names at a time, but because he won't leave me the hell alone. The Larry never does. Gary doesn't so much seem to want to know everything I know as he seems to want to to *question* everything I know. He's maybe five years older than me, white, rocking some truly nerd-classic high pants, and would like me to list the genus and species of every plant we walk past. I definitely remember him from the pre-trip meeting.

But, shit, I remember all of them. No one seems off.

As if sensing my frustration with Gary—usually I'm good at disguising it, but I am a little distracted this time—Diego hangs back in the trail long enough to get Gary's attention and draw it away from me. He makes eye contact with me just long enough for me to think he's doing it on purpose, which confirms my impression of Diego: the solid. Not too loud, not too shy, healthy but not competitive, curious but not annoying, helpful without becoming a nuisance. Diego is solid.

I never know who the solid's going to be until we're out here, so I search for something else memorable about him to prove to myself he was at the pre-trip meeting. And yes, I have it: he wanted to bring some of his own gear. We get that sometimes. Someone with enough outdoorsmanship to have bought their own hiking backpack, tent, etc. wants to use their own stuff instead of ours. We prefer they use ours. How big a fight they put up about it depends less on their experience level and more on their personality. Diego didn't argue once I explained it to him. Now, he draws Gary forward on the trail, pointing out a tree split in half by lightning.

They pass by Landilee to get a closer look. Landilee I remember instantly simply because I had to say her name to myself so many times to get it into my memory. Eventually I used Land O'Lakes butter as a mental trigger to dredge it up. Not that she's plump or otherwise buttery; I just couldn't think of anything else. I haven't been able to figure out what type of name it is. She's of an indeterminate race and age; maybe mixed race or Mediterranean, older than everyone else, probably in her forties or fifties. She has a vaguely mom-like quality about her, though she keeps to herself. I'm not sure yet if she has trouble relating to the other participants or if she just doesn't want to connect. Currently, she's wearing earbuds and walking mid-trail. Her eyes are taking everything in, and she seems content, so that's fine.

Who's left? It takes me a few moments to realize she's behind me, which shows me just how distracted I am. Somehow I actually forgot about the straggler. That's who she is: the straggler. Also known as the chronically unfit. Also also known as the one who doesn't disclose health issues when we ask them to. I've never understood why people do that, but it happens almost every trip no matter how much we stress that we need to know any and all health issues before leaving. We can't turn anyone away, so it's not like they're afraid they won't be allowed. Usually when something rears its head and we ask them why they didn't put it on their medical form the answer is something like, "I'm sorry. I thought it didn't matter."

I can't think of her name right away. Carol? Rory? Brooke, that's it. Knew it had an "r." Brooke is young, white, and overweight. I knew in the first hour of hiking that she hadn't made herself pass the cardio test we recommend to them before signing up for this trip. (Twenty minutes of uninterrupted climbing on the stair machine.) Her cheeks are so red they verge on maroon. It turns out she has a bad ankle she didn't disclose. Or she made up the ankle because she's embarrassed about her lack of endurance. Either way, she's slowing us down.

I turn to her, smiling. "Doing alright Brooke?"

If possible, her flush spreads even more across her cheeks. She's so introverted that any attention from anyone seems to fluster her. "Yes, sure, okay, good."

I pause, letting her catch up to me. It's probably around noon, close to time for lunch. The sun still hasn't shown itself from behind the clouds. "How's the ankle feeling?"

"It hurts," she admits. "But the brace helps."

"I'm glad." I keep one knee brace and one ankle brace in my Oh Shit Bag. We use one or both almost every trip, even if it just ends up being for my own bad knee.

"I'm sorry," she says, not making eye contact with me. "For being slow."

"It's all good. We have plenty of time."

Her breathing is so heavy I wonder if she's about to hyperventilate or have a heart attack, and I do remember her now, from the pre-trip meeting. I could hear her breathing even then, sitting around the table, too strained for being at rest.

"Yeah but I really should've—I really shouldn't have come. I'm so sorry." Now her breathing is wheezy too, and I realize she's about to cry.

"Hey, Brooke, that's not true. It's okay. I'm glad you came."

She stops walking, bends over with her hands on her knees. I glance ahead. The only person looking back is Diego, the solid. He says something to Joey, who turns and looks a question at me. I wave him on, telling him to go ahead. I hear Gary ask him loudly, "What's wrong with that girl?" and wish I could smack him.

I don't watch to see how many participants turn to look at us. Instead, I turn my back to them and step to block their view of Brooke, mostly so she won't see them watching. I trust that Bianca and Joey will get everyone back on track and moving along.

Dropping to a squatted crouch beside Brooke, I keep my hands loose, posture casual as I say to her, "What can I do, Brooke? What's wrong?"

From this angle, I can see that she's not actually crying, which is a relief but also concerning. It means her continued ragged breathing is something else. Heart trouble? Asthma? Panic attack?

She can't or doesn't answer me for several minutes. I stay there, quiet, and tell her it's going to be okay. She keeps her head dropped down but sinks to sit on the ground. "I have... anxiety..." she pants.

"That sucks," I answer, sinking to a seat beside her. "You know, I used to have a dog with anxiety."

She glances up at me, eyes wide and a little confused, but nods once.

"When he got upset he'd just start howling," I told her. "And he had the most ridiculous howl, so we never knew whether to laugh or feel sorry for him."

She lets out a little courtesy snort-chuckle.

I keep talking, telling her about my old shepherd Rhino, and how he used to snore and even bark in his sleep. He also loved tomatoes, which was fucking weird, and eventually came to love my wife over me, which was equal parts traitorous and endearing.

By the time I've finished telling her about the time he ate dishwasher detergent and threw up all over the house, which is definitely one of those stories that's only funny in retrospect knowing he turned out fine, Brooke's breathing has calmed to a non-scary level and she's actually making eye contact with me as we talk. She waits until the story wraps up before saying softly, "Thank you. Not everyone knows what to do when I have one of those."

I shrug. "No problem."

"Do you have a family member or someone with anxiety?"

"We've had other participants with it before."

She looks hopeful. "Really?"

"For sure. Everyone's got something."

Her eyes are glassy. I reach out to touch her arm, to help her stand so we can catch up with the others. She's nodding a lot to herself, grateful, I think, to feel like she belongs. I freeze with my hand hovering in the air. *Does* she belong?

I turn my reach toward her into reaching for my boots. I untie and retie the laces, looking down, stalling while I try to swallow my fear—or at least keep it off my face. It could be her. Brooke could be the extra. And I've put myself alone with her.

I don't want it to be her. Which makes me realize I've been assuming that she isn't. But what I want doesn't have anything to do with it. One of these participants *is* the eleventh, and why wouldn't it be Brooke? Because I like her? Feel sorry for her?

Maybe she feels like she doesn't belong because she doesn't.

Maybe she's having trouble controlling her body, her emotions, and her reactions because they're not really hers, because this set of human materials is unfamiliar to her—new.

Standing, I look ahead toward the now-empty trail the rest of the group has disappeared down. "You ready to keep going?" I ask her.

For a moment, I'm actually too afraid to turn around and look at her. I'm vividly, intensely convinced that what I'll see won't be Brooke at all. It will be a tall, dark, thin figure that's almost a person, but not quite. I don't want to see.

Her voice comes small and unsteady. "Yeah, okay. Sure. Thanks."

I look at her. Still her. I force a smile, but I can feel

that it doesn't look true. "Let's hit it then. I bet they've stopped for lunch up a ways. I'm starving."

I wait, gesturing for her to walk ahead of me. It's the courteous thing to do—the thing I'd always do. Walk behind to be sure her ankle holds, that she's really okay. I tell myself that's why I do it now.

I tell myself it's not because I'm afraid to have her at my back.

# RULE #7: FIX LITTLE ISSUES TO PREVENT BIG PROBLEMS

THE GROUP HAS STOPPED to eat. Our lunches are almost always food that doesn't need to be cooked so we don't have to set up the camp stove. Today everyone is eating peanut butter and honey tortilla wraps, which has to be one of the dumber meals we've put together. I think this one was Joey's doing. At least everyone also gets a pouch of dried fruit and a protein bar. The cool thing about newbs, though, is that they don't care. They don't know any different, and to them every part of this is an adventure—even the lame lunch.

Bianca has gathered up everyone's water bottles and taken them down to the stream to refill with the filter. Everyone else sits around a widening in the trail, clumped in little clusters of twos, threes, and fours, chatting happily about cool things they can see nearby or that they've just seen on the trail. The only person sitting alone is Landilee, which makes sense, because she still has her earbuds in. Not exactly welcoming. When Brooke and I walk up, Gary immediately perks. "What happened?" he asks loud enough for everyone to hear. Because he's nosy, the Larry, or because he's suspicious, the extra?

"Everything's fine," I say evasively. "How's everybody's feet doing? This is usually about the time when people start realizing where their blisters are going to be."

No one asks me for moleskin, but once I pull it out of my bag and start cutting it up, Meg and Diego admit that putting some on wouldn't hurt. Diego scratches at his arm as he holds his hand out for it. He scratches more as he applies it, scraping around his jacket sleeve enough that peeling the sticky backing off the material is difficult. Finally, I gesture to his arm and say, "Got a bug bite or something going on there?"

"What?" He looks up at me, then down where his own fingers dig into his forearm. "Oh. I don't know." He undoes the Velcro tightening his jacket at the cuff and works several layers of sleeves up.

There's a rash on his arm, on the underside, between wrist and elbow. It's small, a little larger than a blotchy quarter, with raised edges that look almost like a grid. What makes it weird is the color. It's not pink, not even purple, but almost blue. It kind of looks like veins popping up from the skin, but of course veins don't cluster and round like that. Veins don't itch, either.

Something is wrong.

I look at him, trying to hide my reaction, my primal revulsion. Is it telling me to stay away from that rash, or from *him*?

"What *is* that?" Diego asks, eyes wide. The fingers of his other hand hover over it, like he wants to keep scratching but suddenly doesn't want to touch it, either. His reaction makes me feel a bit better about him, at least. I still want nothing to do with that round spot.

"Some sort of rash," I mutter, trying not to draw the attention of the other participants. "It itches?"

"Yeah."

"Joey, would you dig out the cortisone for us?" To Diego I say, "Maybe you brushed against something on the trail. It happens. We'll put some cream on it, and it'll probably go down soon. Just keep an eye on it and let me know if it gets worse, okay?"

"Okay," he says, but his voice is slightly high and creaky. I get it. It's unnerving to have something wrong with your body, especially something unknown. But he's the solid, so I'm pretty sure he'll be alright. I can probably at least trust him to actually let me know if it gets worse and not keep it a secret until his arm falls off or whatever the fuck. People are just so weird about speaking up about things.

While Joey's digging out the small tube of cream, my eyes land on Gary. He has a book open in his lap. A huge, hard-backed, textbook-sized book. He sits on a small rock, both feet flat on the ground, knees together, the book balanced on his thighs. He's leaned so far forward over the book it looks like he'll topple. He slides a finger down the left page like he's looking for something.

I'm still staring at him in dumbfounded bewilderment when he looks up and catches my gaze. "You were wrong earlier about the mulberry bush, Matt. The berries were smaller and gathered in clusters, so it's actually a Callicarpa."

"Gary, where did you get that book?"

He closes it, keeping his place with one hand, and holds it up so I can see the cover. *Flora of the Ozarks and Surrounding Areas: A History and Encyclopedia.* "I bought it."

"Don't you remember us telling y'all to pack light? Nothing you don't need?"

"But I do need it. Identifying plant life is a big part of the reason I came."

"That book must weigh five pounds. You didn't think about taking pictures and IDing them when you got home?"

He shrugs. "I like to know."

I'm usually really good at hiding any annoyance on trips, but this one's an effort. Eventually, the ridiculousness gets to me, and I end up having to hide a smile rather than a sigh. "You do you, Gary."

"Who else would I do?" he asks, and his tone is so flat I can't tell if he's joking or not.

I shake my head and turn away, asking Joey to go down to the water with me to help Bianca bring all the bottles back up. They are a lot to carry at once after they're full, but I really just want an excuse to talk with my trip leaders alone.

As we head toward the area Bianca used to get down to the water, I feel eyes on my back. The urge to turn and look is strong. So strong I almost whirl to catch who's watching me, but that'd be weird. But I can't bear to not look, either. Finally, as I squat to lower myself over a little ledge, I casually glance over my shoulder.

No one is watching me.

When I turn back, my face catches spiderweb. I flinch against it, but I need my hands to keep my balance, so I have to leave the strands there.

As we scuttle down the steep embankment toward the water, Bianca startles and whirls, a hand on her chest, the other clutching an open bottle. Some of the water splashes out, soaking her pant leg. "Shit," she hisses.

My eyebrows shoot up at the profanity, only because Bianca hardly ever cusses. "Sorry. Didn't mean to startle you." I pull at the web stuck to my face.

She looks past us, to where the ledge looms behind us. "It's okay. Just jumpy."

Joey walks right to her and gently takes the bottle from her hand. "Me too." There's something about the softness of his touch, or the admittance in his tone that strikes me as tender. Romantic, even. Are they a thing? They wouldn't be the first couple to pair up from my student staff, but I'm a little surprised I didn't know already. Or maybe they're not yet. Maybe Joey's really just that unnerved.

How could he not be?

"How many you got left?" I ask her, trying to stop rubbing at the invisible strands on my face. She points to three bottles to one side, the filled ones clustered opposite. I hold my hand out for the filter, and she gives it to me, Joey silently taking the bottle from her and capping the lid.

I roll up my sleeves and work for a few minutes, none of us speaking. After the first bottle is done, I ask them, "Any ideas on which one it is?"

Neither of them asks me what I mean. I guess it's all any of us can think about.

Bianca says, "Why, so we can leave them behind?"

"No," I snap, annoyed at the accusation in her tone, because I feel the same way. But what the fuck am I supposed to do here? I force myself to ease my defensiveness. "So we can figure out what the hell is going on and keep everyone safe."

She won't look at me, tugging at her sleeves, but she quietly says, "Rowley." Her tone is drenched in guilt.

"The showoff? Why?"

She shrugs. "He looks most like the thing in the picture. Tall, thin, dark."

Joey frowns at her. "So because he's black? That's profiling."

"That's not what I just said, and you know it." She

gestures to herself as if to drive home a reminder that she herself is black. "Don't push me, Joey."

He puts both hands in the air, taking a step back. "I'm just saying. We're all dark with rain gear on, and even Rowley isn't tall enough to have been that figure."

"He's right about that," I say, screwing the lid on the second to last bottle, my hands frigid from the stream water. I'm also thinking about the fact that Rowley stands out. He intentionally and constantly calls attention to himself. Wouldn't it make more sense for the extra to try to blend in? To hang back, stay quiet? "Whoever it is, they don't look now how they did then. If that even was them. It."

Bianca shrugs. The gesture looks angry, but I know she's just scared. "That's all I can think of. How else can we tell? I remember everyone."

Joey and I nod in unison.

Hedging, Joey volunteers, "Maybe it's Gary."

I put the filter into the last bottle. "Why Gary?"

"He's so *weird*, man."

"That's profiling," Bianca quips, just to make her point.

Joey presses on. "Don't you think he's super weird?"

I do. "Well, yeah. But people are weird. We always have a few weirdos." The idea of picking the person who least fits in is terrifying to me. Like some jacked up popularity contest. It can't come down to that, can it?

Joey shakes his head. "It's not just that kind of weird. Constantly asking 'what's this' and 'what's that' like he's never seen a freaking tree before. And he doesn't talk normal, or interact with anyone right. It's like he's not familiar with... anything. Like he's new here."

His use of 'new here' sends the gooseflesh already on my wet wrists crawling all the way up under my jacket, over my forearms and elbows. The residue from the spiderweb still clings to my skin, making me long to rub at it even though my hands are full.

I cap the last bottle. "Diego has a weird rash." I point to my prickling skin, fingertips dripping onto my jacket. "Here."

"You think it's Diego?" Joey asks.

I shrug, drying my hands on a handkerchief before working them into my gloves. "Could be. If it's trying to blend in, he'd be a good choice. Or maybe he touched it."

Bianca blinks at me several times, hugging her torso, rocking back and forth to stay warm. It gets cold quick when you stop moving. The sun has yet to break through the clouds. The air smells like old rain. "Touched the... the extra person and got a rash?"

I shrug helplessly, arms out. "The only other person I've wondered about so far is Brooke. She had a panic attack back there, when y'all went ahead. And she's cool, but it made me wonder."

"Wonder what?" Joey asks, leaning in.

"How are we going to be able to tell who it is when

we don't even know *what* it is, or what it wants?" I can hear the fear in my own voice, and I clamp my jaw.

I can't give into fear. They need me to be the leader here. If only they knew how young I feel right this moment, how unlike an adult. I remember my dad admitting to me once that he still doesn't feel like an adult—that none of us do and we're all just faking it. I have the brief thought of going to Landilee or Gary, the two who seem older than me, and asking them for help as if I were a kid lost in a store. As if age alone actually guarantees anything. But of course, either one of them could be the extra. Best case, I'd be worrying a participant about something beyond their control. Worst case, I'd be telling the extra we're onto it *and* admitting we have no idea what to do.

Bianca begins gathering up some of the filled bottles, sliding straps over her wrists and tucking others into her largest pockets. "I've been thinking about that too. I think we'll know."

Joey says, "What do you mean, we'll know? Like we'll know it when we see it kind of thing?"

*Something is wrong*. It seems like Bianca has gotten past total denial. She still isn't on board with leaving anyone behind, but at least she's stopped trying to argue that there's some easy answer we've missed.

"No," she says. We gather bottles too. "I mean I think we'll know what it wants soon enough. Because whatever that is, it's going to try to get it before long. To take it. And then we'll know."

The water over the pulse in my wrists has left me cold, jittery. I'll warm up when we start moving.

As the three of us head back to the group—I've never left participants unattended so many times in all my years—I look up toward the top of the trail above us. And leaning over, looking down as if peering into the depths of a well, it's Jo who I see first, their wide, dark eyes studying us curiously.

The ghost of the web still clings to my face.

# RULE #8: MINIMIZE CAMPFIRE IMPACTS

WE SIT around our campfire that night, finishing the first hot meal of the trip. I feel like I've been holding my breath all day. I've tried not to seem too hawk-eyed, but I'm watching every move everyone makes, analyzing it, comparing it with what I would do and what I remember about that person, trying to pinpoint motives—to excavate hidden agendas. My wife would be better at this than I am. We'll get home from some event, and she'll point out to me micro-behaviors that specific people did and what they probably meant. I see them once she draws attention to them, but on my own I'm a much more face-value guy.

Thinking of her brings on an intense wash of missing her. I ache to walk in and see her sprawled on the sofa reading, for her to follow me around as I unpack, asking me about how the trip went, to finally hug her tight after my first shower in days. I try not to think about her when I'm out here. It sounds unromantic, I know, but I can't be homesick while I'm on the job, and I'm too busy. With no cell signal, I can't call her before bed or anything anyway, so it's best to think about her as little as possible. It makes the time pass quicker. Still, sometimes I slip. I'll see a critter she would love to watch or hear one of the participants tell a joke that I make a mental note to remember—one that'll make her laugh.

This is the first time, though, that thinking of her and how I miss her brings with it a deep, sharp pang of fear.

It's worse that I don't know what it's for. Fear of what, exactly? She's safe at home. I might be in danger, but I have no way of knowing even that for sure. No one has threatened anything. I don't know what's wrong, exactly—only that something most definitely is.

I feel doubly resolved that we can't bring the extra home with us. We can't expose everyone to whatever this is. I want her and everyone I care about far, far away from the extra. I want her safe.

The feeling is so strong that I actually pull out my cell phone and power it on, despite knowing there will be no signal. I keep my movements calm in the darkness beyond the fire's ring of light so none of the participants ask me what's up. As expected, it's not of any use.

Bianca holds the trash open for everyone to

dispose of their leavings. We encourage everyone to eat as much as possible, both because they need the energy out here and because it means less for us to pack out. Joey brings out graham crackers, marshmallows, and chocolate bars. I stifle a groan. I think I used to actually like s'mores, but I can no longer remember why. That feels like several lifetimes ago. Still, it's the most-requested food at the pre-trip meetings. Pratik, our foreign exchange student, has never had one and is super excited. He thinks of them as an American classic.

So I play along, trying to hide my growing sense of dread, and show him how to roast a marshmallow. It spurs a discussion of technique. Meg, the pretty one, asserts that the best thing to do is shove it directly into the flame until it catches fire, and then blow it out. Surprisingly, it's Landilee, the quiet mom-ish one, who argues. She thinks the char makes it taste burnt. She's all about the slow roast, rotating frequently and never letting the marshmallow touch the flame so that it warms all the way through but doesn't blacken. Pratik is enraptured by this all. He burns his first one so badly we all make him throw it away. He drops his second one into the coals when it gets too plump and gooey. Finally, he finishes a third and builds his s'more, leaning forward and taking a huge bite.

We all grow silent as we watch him chew. When he finally swallows, he makes a *guh* sound and exclaims, "Water! That is *so sweet*."

Everyone laughs as he scrambles for his water bottle. But after several big gulps, he does finish the messy square, complete with licking his fingers.

During the giggling and 'mallow roasting, I notice Jo scratching the side of their neck. It draws my attention because they have to work their hand into the layers around their throat in order to scratch, which makes a swishing, rustling sound against their gear.

Is Jo the extra? Or did they touch the extra? Or did they touch Diego—or is that the same thing? Hell, maybe Jo had a rash first and Diego touched them. I consider touching Diego's rash to see if I get one, but fuck that. I've been watching people all day, but touches can be so casual I might have looked right at one and failed to notice it.

Then again, maybe Jo's neck just itches.

Once everyone has had at least one s'more and fallen into quiet, someone letting out a companionable burp, Pratik asks the group, "Does anyone have any creeps?"

Everyone is silent for a heartbeat or two, probably trying to puzzle out what he means, but I can tell by the conspiratorial relish in his voice. I say, "You mean ghost stories?"

He nods happily, the firelight reflecting up on his face to give him the classic campfire underlit glow. "Yes, like in the movies."

Some of the participants chuckle, repeating it to each other. "Any creeps?" But it's fond, not teasing. This is part of what most of them come for—the sense of camaraderie. Meg is the first to offer up a story, and it's the classic killer's hook on the car handle one. It involves more laughter than fear, although there's a certain tension in the air simply from being outside in an unfamiliar place in the dark—a certain inherent atmosphere imbued in a group of people around a campfire.

Next up is Gary, who does a terrifically horrible job telling the one about the man who lets his dog lick his hand at night when he gets scared, with the twist ending being a madman who can lick hands too. I've heard it several times, but Gary's telling is so bogged down by mundanities that by the time he gets to the punch line, which he mangles, several people have started yawning. Jo is still scratching at their neck, and I see Bianca notice it too.

Finally, Landilee speaks up with a tale. It's one I haven't heard. It starts off with the standard, "This is a true story," but then it unravels into something just uncanny enough to actually unnerve me. It's not so much what actually happens—an unusually large and faceless man follows her around sporadically throughout her life since childhood, pressing himself to windows and doors—but the way she tells it. Most people start with, "This actually happened," but they say it happened to someone they know, and then it devolves into vagaries and plot holes. Landilee says it happened to her, and she has just enough extraneous details—the settings and exact appearances of the man—to make it feel real. Maybe it's also because she's older. She lends it the cadence not of kids at a slumber party, but of an adult telling you something you need to understand is true.

I'm watching not her, but the others as she finishes her story. Joey catches my gaze with wide eyes, and I think it's not just the story that's scared him, but the fact that she's telling it. We try to keep things light on our trips. We want everyone to have fun. No politics, religion, or upsetting things. This story crosses the line from fun campfire tale over into actually unsettling.

Landilee has everyone's attention as she says, "And he still comes to me, every once in a while. Not often. But I'll wake up in the middle of the night and see him standing, silhouetted behind my curtains, or waiting outside a door with frosted glass. I think, more than anything, he just wants to be let in. He just wants to belong."

Chills.

Breathless, I don't know what to say. I waited too long—should've derailed this story sooner.

Finally, Rowley says, "But what happened?"

Landilee turns her head to him, and I realize she's been holding it perfectly still until now. "What do you mean?"

His voice is angry. "At the end of the story? What happened to 'you' and the man?"

She shrugs. "It's not a story. It really happens to me. And I guess it doesn't have an end yet. I guess it will end when I die or... or he gets in."

Meg lets out a little gasp that sounds perilously

like a sob. "But what about when you aren't inside? What about now, when you're just out in the open?"

Landilee shrugs.

Rowley scowls so hard the firelight turns the lines of his face into cartoon relief. "That's a shitty story."

"Hey," I reprimand, but I tend to agree. It is an especially shitty story to tell out here right before bed. She should be experienced enough to know that hers wasn't in line with the other types of stories being told. I study Landilee, wondering what kind of person she is. I don't know her. I remember her from the pre-trip meeting, but I remember everyone. Some of those memories are false. Someone here is not who they seem.

Pratik says softly, "I am a creep."

Startled, I look to him. It's as if he's just answered my train of thought. But of course, he can't know what I'm thinking. Can he? If the extra is powerful enough to change our memories, then maybe they're also powerful enough to read our thoughts. I shift in my folding chair, moving my gaze from face to face, looking for anyone looking too hard at me.

Of course, it's probably just Pratik's English that's off, not him. Probably. *I am a creep* could easily mean *I am afraid*. If he were the extra, surely he wouldn't just announce it like that? Unless he's toying with us, with me. Unless he's enjoying watching me squirm.

Does anyone have any creeps?

*Yes, Pratik*, I think, watching him for a tell-tale

reaction to my thoughts despite how stupid it makes me feel. *We have one creep, for sure.*

He shows no indication of even noticing my attention on him. I'm not sure if that makes me feel better or worse. If it's not him, then who is it?

And what the fuck are we going to do about it?

# RULE #9: STICK TO THE PLAN

I LIE AWAKE LISTENING, thinking, waiting. I'm listening to Joey alternate between dry wheezing and soft snoring, but I'm trying to hear beyond it. In the outdoors there's never any shortage of sounds. Usually I tune them out, because paying attention to each crack and rustle will keep me up all night, but tonight I can't tune out anything. Wired. I'm thinking about what Bianca said, about how we'll know what the extra wants soon enough. *It's going to try to get it*, she'd said. And that, I guess, is what I'm waiting for. For it to try to take whatever it is it wants.

For hours, I picture one of the eight participants creeping out of their tent. I listen for zippers, undisguisable no matter how slowly drawn. I envision horrible fates for all of us, for the ten. I see a different face on each nightmare creation of my imagining, and each is terrible in its own way.

I don't sleep. I never even close my eyes. I briefly

consider waking the trip leaders to take shifts with me, but I know I won't be able to sleep even if they're awake, so they might as well rest. I lie in dread, trying to prepare myself for every eventuality. Trying to envision myself stopping the extra, defending my trip leaders, saving the participants. I try to foresee so I can protect. I try to understand what it wants so I can stop it from getting it.

At three in the morning, I get up and quietly leave the tent to check the campsite. I walk softly through the dead, damp leaves, make sure all the tents remain zipped and sound, triple check that the fire hasn't simmered back to life, and scan for anything out of place. There's the creak of trees, the soft rustling of people shifting in their sleeping bags. The smell of charred wood, the taste of fall in the air. All seems normal.

The air is cold where it wedges its fingers under my collar. I tip my head back and look up at the sky, my breath steaming upward in a sigh of condensation. Some of the clouds have finally cleared away, leaving the sky in brilliant patchwork. The expanse of the night is awesome out here. The darkness stretches from the ground up and out, like it's getting sucked into the empty space between stars. The constellations between cloud cover are vivid without light pollution, moving subtly in a way I never notice back home. Stars aren't objects, not exactly. They hover out there, and the light they beam down bends and warps on its way through our atmosphere, making it look like they twinkle. An illusion.

From the corner of my eye, I catch the short tail of a shooting star. It's gone before I can really watch.

The cold has slithered under my skin. I get back in the tent, sleeping bag scarcely warm, and continue to wait.

Dawn blooms ever closer, still misty and gray beyond the shifting clouds, and my fingers are hovering over the buttons on my watch so that when the alarm beeps, it's silenced with an amputated squeak. Joey stirs but doesn't wake.

Again, I climb from the tent and survey the campsite. Everything's the same, undisturbed. Still.

I'm exhausted, terrified, chewed up by my own doubt. My head swims with *should have*s and *should still*s and *what if*s that do no good. I know nothing more than I did before. Nothing has changed.

I pack up what I can, light the camp stove, and wait. *We'll know what it wants, soon enough.*

*Something's wrong.*

The sun rises. Bianca and Joey are the first to emerge, as they should be. They go silently about their morning business, the sets of their shoulders and heads letting me know how they feel. I need to get them home, out of this. I hope there is an out of this. I hope to be able to worry about how it's affected them. I hope that eventually I'll be able to call them into my office and see how they're coping. Next comes Bianca's tentmates, Brooke and Landilee. I study them, tracing their movements, watching for abnormalities or clues.

The others emerge by ones and twos, sleepy and subdued. None of them look sinister in the morning dim. None of them act strangely. None of them seem to have hidden agendas.

The only thing I notice is that now, in addition to Diego and Jo, Meg and Gary are also scratching conspicuously. Meg itches at her collarbone, Gary at his shin. I watch the others specifically for scratching but see none. My own skin prickles with itches—invisible hot spots that I long to dig fingers into. It's like finding out someone you sat next to has lice. Every place where my clothes rub my skin feels like it could be a rash. Every place where it doesn't feels like it might become one. I refuse to let myself start scratching. I feel on the brink of something, like if I start I might not be able to stop.

We eat a quick breakfast so we can hit the trail. We're not dangerously low on food—happy stomachs make happy hikers—but we are lower than normal. No thirds, and only some people get seconds. There's an extra mouth to feed.

This time as we set out the tone is more somber, and I'm not sure if it's because I'm setting it or if everyone is just tired. We're all sore, that's for sure. My shoulders protest when I haul on my pack, and my legs ache from yesterday. The participants groan and grumble, but we break camp and start making progress.

After about an hour we come to a spot where we cross another section of trail. This particular hike is the outside loop of a deformed figure 8, with the belt of the 8 serving as a possible shortcut. Taking the belt instead of staying with the longer path would shave an entire day and night off our trip time.

The group is trudging ahead, Bianca having led them right past it per our plan, but I stop, thinking. We could turn here and be back today. No more nights out here. No more waiting. Just... home.

The wish to be home dropkicks me. Out of here, gone. Safe. Like this never happened.

I could call ahead, bring them back, make up some reason for us to end early and head back right now.

But what would we do when we got to the van? Who would we let in it, and how would we choose?

I still don't know who the extra is. As desperately as I wish I were not here, doing this, we need more time. More time to figure out who is coming home with us.

Sucking in a breath so deep it strains my rib muscles against my backpack, I follow after the group.

As we head to the reward vista of our trip, we pass an older couple on their way down. I hear our folks saying hi one at a time as they make their way to the back of our line, and my mind races. My first thought is that I could tell them, a shot of hope. Maybe they have a satellite phone that works, or could, what? Send for help? Send who, to do what, exactly? Even if they didn't think I was delusional, I can't imagine what they could do.

This all flashes through my mind as my group's greetings grow farther back, closer to me where I bring up the rear.

Finally, Brooke lets out a squeaky hello, and then it's me. I look at them, a fit pair in their sixties or seventies, decked in nice gear and clearly used to this terrain. They have bright, open faces, and do the trail nod. Just a couple of friendly strangers.

My own forced smile freezes on my face as the thought occurs to me that they, too, could be extras. Whatever that is. Did one person set out on a hike alone, only to head back with a partner they remember always having?

"Hello," says the man, and I nod, voice gone in my swirl of thoughts.

Or will they head back home with three?

"Hi," the lady chirps, waving a hand in a little salute.

The idea of our extra splitting from us, following them instead of us—it gives me hope, an imagined relief, and then guilt for even wishing they'd leave us alone and become someone else's problem.

I look back over my shoulder at them, headed downhill, and realize I never responded to their greetings. My throat feels dry, too thick to swallow. Was that an opportunity? It had passed so fast. Did I miss it, dodge it, or had it never really been for me at all?

# RULE #10: KNOW YOUR TRIP

THE VISTA IS a high bluff that overlooks a beautiful swatch of land exploding with fall foliage. The sun has finally fully come out, casting everything in fiery brilliance. It's the consolation for sore thighs and swollen feet and screaming backs. We always stop here for lunch. Today, it's the first time people have felt warm enough to take off their hats and shed a layer or two, and suddenly everyone looks different. The first costume change in two days plus unfamiliar faces make for the uncanny feeling that everyone in the group has been swapped. Even Bianca and Joey look a little different with their hat hair and somber expressions.

As Joey gets everyone situated with lunch, Bianca pulls out the program's digital camera and starts snapping shots. It reminds me of the picture with the figure that we think was the extra, that first night by the stream, and gives me an idea.

I power on my own phone and tell the group I'm doing some mini-interviews for social media. One by one, I video them, and I ask the same set of questions: "Why are you here with us? What do you want?" One by one, they answer.

Rowley: "I'm here to have fun. What do I want? Tacos! Or a monster burrito. Ooo, or a loaded burger with fries."

Meg: "I wanted to spend time with Jo, and to push myself to do something new."

Jo: "I want a group where I feel like I belong."

Landilee: "I'm here to spend time in nature, see the beauty of this area."

Brooke: "I don't know. I want a shower."

Gary: "I wanted to study the life here, to identify different species."

Diego: "I just want to be around people, enjoy myself."

Pratik: "I came to learn more about this culture."

Of course, I overanalyze each answer, but my real intention is the playback. After I've recorded them all, I step aside and watch it all on mute, searching for shadows or lights or other weirdness, but everything looks the same. Just eight strangers when there should be seven.

While everyone takes turns with the toilet paper before our second half of the day hiking, I step aside and make a video to send to my wife. "Hey babe, it's me. I just wanted to say hi, and I miss you." I realize I'm close to tearing up, and I don't know why I'm sending it. In case, I guess, I don't make it back to her. Shorter will go through easier anyway. I smile, blinking behind my sunglasses. "I love you, and I can't wait to be back home." I still don't have enough bars, but when I'm done I push send, knowing that my phone will keep trying, and that if it grabs a signal here and there it might eventually get through.

We hit the trail, headed downhill toward our final campsite, and on a whim, I ask Joey, "Joey, why are you out here?"

He rolls his eyes at me. "Because you're paying me."

"Fair enough. Bianca?"

She shakes her head at me, holding a hand up as if to block her face.

# RULE #11: KNOW YOUR PEOPLE

LYING in my tent on our final night, sleep is a joke with no punchline. My mind, a mouse in a maze.

I can't stop thinking about how Bianca covered her face when I tried to video her. I've watched it back several times, and I can see her face before she raises her hand. It looks normal. Not tall, dark, and shadowy. But it has made the loose thread irresistible, and I can't help tugging on it.

Why have I been so sure that Bianca and Joey aren't options?

I'm not sure. That's the answer. It's just the most practical thing, to assume they're not. No, not most practical. Easiest.

I don't want the extra to be one of them, but couldn't it be? If whatever this is comes with false memories that seem as real to me as all the others, who's to say that those memories couldn't go deeper, be more extensive? I remember Bianca and Joey from work. I remember hiring them—each of them—and training them. I remember evaluating them at the end of each semester, and times that they came to me with various problems and ideas. I remember when they made trip leader, and when we scheduled them on this trip. I remember them.

But I remember everybody here.

How deep could invented memories go? Years back like that?

Longer?

How do I know that *any* of my memories are real?

How do I even know that I have any real memories at all—that they aren't all invented?

What if *I'm* the fucking extra?

Hours pass, me thinking myself sick, getting nowhere, eyes and ears open to anything suspicious from camp. I keep wondering if it will show itself, do something. *We'll know what it wants, soon enough.*

But we haven't, and we don't. And what if we won't?

It strikes me, sharply, that this is even more horrible.

We may not be able to tell what it wants. It might not want anything spectacular. It might want nothing more than to blend in, to fit in, to come home with us.

I realize on the heels of that thought that although I was dreading it making a move of some kind, I was also depending on it. I've been counting on it showing its hand so I can stop it.

It might not show its hand at all.

Somewhere within the last hour of night, I must have fallen asleep, because when I wake up I have a brief and wonderful feeling that it's all been a bizarre restless nightmare. None of it has happened, and it's the first night, and there are ten people here, not eleven. I'm not losing my mind, and everyone is safe.

But as I haul myself into wakefulness, dressing and packing up my tent, the illusion drops away, and I am mired in this awful reality that can't be real but is.

"Matt?"

I jolt, whirling so abruptly that I knock the mug from Bianca's hands. She gasps and I blurt, "Shit, sorry." I pick up the fallen dish, lined with coffee. "Sorry. I was thinking. I'll get you some more."

She shakes her head at me, her fear so plain it makes me stand, pulling her aside so the participants can't catch sight of her face. "It's okay. I wasn't even drinking it, just holding it."

"You sure?" When she nods, I say, "Joey?"

He lifts his head in that half-nod acknowledgement.

"Will you come help us filter water?"

"Sure thing, boss."

We all walk around gathering water bottles from the participants. At each, I stare intently into their face, searching for something. Anything.

But there's nothing.

Hands clenched, I lead my two staff down to the water to talk.

At the muddy bank, I let them do the filtering as I pace. I glance down the path to make sure no participants have trailed along within hearing distance. "We're out of time," I tell them. It's the last day. We're back to and past where the figure 8 cut across. "We have about three hours, four if we're slow, before we reach the van. We have to make a decision. We can't bring home eleven people. Practically, morally. We can't."

Joey gazes up at me, alarmed. "But what decision? What can we do?"

"We'll do what we have to do. Only ten people are getting in that van."

Bianca whispers, "We can't leave someone, Matt."

"Honestly, y'all. No joking, no accusations. Do either of you have a better idea?" I keep my eyes on theirs so they know it's a genuine question and not passive aggression.

Joey shakes his head.

Bianca sounds terrified when she says, "We just can't."

That's it. No bright ideas, no better options. My heart is racing. I can't quite believe it, but I'm saying it. Firmly, authoritatively, so they know this isn't a request anymore. "We have to."

She won't meet my eyes. Accusatory, and I don't blame her for it. If I'm wrong, this is on me. All of this is on me, and I don't want it, but what other choice do I have?

I consider, once again, that I might be losing my mind, but if I'm experiencing delusions so complete and intricate that I'm hallucinating that my trip leaders are experiencing it too, what the fuck am I supposed to do about it? Besides, I know I'm not. It's a thing I know, like whether I'm awake. A philosopher might be able to argue their way around it, but the truth is some things you just know. I'm not losing it. This is happening.

"How will we decide?" Joey asks, and I'm struck not by the question itself, but by the fact that he's not arguing with me. He, too, can feel that this is bad, wrong, and he's already accepted that we'll have to make this choice. I'm surprised it's Bianca who's wading through denial and not him.

"Yeah," Bianca echoes, sounding less determined and more like she's still trying to talk me out of it. "We remember everyone, so that means one of those memories doesn't count. It means any one of them could be the. . . planted one. It could be anyone. It could be one of us."

"That doesn't do us any good," I say flatly. "I went down that rabbit hole last night, to no use. If it's one of us three who already know about it, we're fucked."

She looks down.

"You're right," I soften. "You're totally right. But we can't operate under that type of thinking, can we? We have to assume we can stick together, the three of us. It's not me. Is it one of you?"

They both shake their heads vigorously, eyes wide as deer.

"Then I believe you. I have to." But her words have unnerved me. The thought of Joey or Bianca being the extra makes me less scared than sad. To think that they're not real, that their growth and histories and experiences don't count.

I shake my head. I can't believe that. If it's one of them, there's nothing I can do about it now; I've already told them everything I know.

"What if we ask the whole group?" Joey asks. "Actually tell them what's going on. See if talking about it with everyone shakes something loose?"

I pause, considering. "It might lead to panic. At least arguing. And I'm not sure a group decision is really better than the three of us?"

Bianca is shaking her head. "No. It would be groupthink. Everyone accusing Gary, probably. The weirdest, or the least favorite."

I agree. The idea of what metrics people might use to decide was terrifying to me. Arbitrary at best, cruel at worst. I could see Brooke being left behind in a literal footrace, or Jo being ostracized, or Pratik.

Joey says, "Yeah. You're right. I was just thinking."

"Then how will we pick?" Bianca asks again. I appreciate the *we*, intentional or not.

I swallow, take in a breath, swallow again. "We'll come back together in three hours. The three of us. Before we get to the van. We'll have to take a vote."

"A vote."

"Yeah. Both of you, watch. Think. Choose. We'll vote."

I would welcome another argument, or at least a suggestion, but none come.

None of us say anything else as we finish filtering the water.

# RULE #12: YOU'RE A LEADER, NOT A GUIDE

IN THE PAST, I've been naturally calm during crisis. When I need to be level-headed in times of chaos, I have a sort of zone I slip into that cuts off the stress and lets me think. I haven't gotten there yet this time. The only thinking I can do is useless, circular. I feel like there must be something I've missed, something I fucked up, some way out of this impossible thing. But the more I let in panic the less effective I become at leading, and these people need me to lead them now. It's more than I signed up for, but if I don't step up, I'm putting everyone at risk.

I go into crisis mode now, shutting off emotion with a hard switch, allowing only logic and fact to come through.

Process of elimination. It's the only way.

I know it's not me. I have to choose to believe it's not Bianca or Joey. All of my knowledge is incomplete, so I stop the little voice that shouts at me, *That's not enough!*

Since four participants have rashes, and not just one, I assume they got them from the extra, which means none of them are the extra. That rules out Diego, Jo, Meg, and Gary.

Rowley, Pratik, Brooke, and Landilee remain. The show-off, the international student, the straggler, and the mom-vibes loner.

As we leave our final campsite, Pratik stops to take a picture and Rowley, once again, makes fun of his selfie stick. He stands behind Pratik, getting in his shot, and makes a dumb face while pretending to hold up his own invisible phone extender.

"You know what," bursts out quiet little Jo, "methinks the lady doth protest too much."

We all look at them, surprised, because they've been one of the most cheerful presences on this trip so far. Rowley looks at them, not sure whether to scowl or laugh yet. "Huh?"

"Me*thinks*," Jo drawls out, "the *lady*," pointing to Rowley, "is protesting a little too much."

"Who are you calling a lady... dude?"

Jo's cheeks flush hot orange.

Oh, fuck. This is not what we need. I need to be focusing on who it might be, not everyone behaving themselves.

Jo says, "For someone who's not into selfie sticks, you sure do talk about Pratik's a lot."

Rowley, making a face of exaggerated disinterest, shrugs. "They're lame."

"Why don't you try it." It isn't a question; it's a challenge.

Pratik, looking a little frightened, follows the exchange with unease. Jo asks him, "Can Rowley borrow your gizmo?"

"Pratik," I interject, "you don't have to let anyone use it. Guys, let's just—"

"I don't mind," he says quietly, handing it to Rowley. He even shows the much taller young man how to use it.

Rowley holds it up, extending his arm to get his head and upper body in the shot. He pulls a duck face, clowning, and throws up a peace sign. Then he takes a few more, dropping a few of the antics and actually, it seems, trying to get a good shot. Finally, he lifts the front of his shirt and jacket to show his abs, snapping several more.

We all watch in a strange sort of breathless silence.

Finally, Rowley exclaims, "Daaaaaaaaang! Selfie sticks are awesome!"

We all burst into laughter. I feel a wash of relief. In other groups, that might've gotten bad.

Rowley gives the stick back to Pratik with a brief, "Sorry, man. You were right," and the trip leaders urge everyone on. Pratik wears a quiet, self-satisfied smile.

I like them. I like them all. Even Gary, who interrupts my thoughts to ask me about the birdcall he heard just now. I guess he didn't pack his bird book.

I don't want any of them to be the extra, but want doesn't have anything to do with it.

Only ten of us are going home.

# RULE #13: DON'T PANIC

OVER THE NEXT two and a half hours, I scour them for clues.

I even take a group selfie using the program camera, hoping to spot some anomaly on the small screen that I couldn't see in person or on my phone. There's nothing. No more shadowy shape, no glowing eyes or visible rashes or missing people. Just eleven smiling faces.

I'm left with four options and no provable way to eliminate any, so now I'm down to hunches. I ignore the part of me that's freaking the hell out about the fact that hunches are not nearly good enough to make this kind of a decision. This decision, at the very least, will change my life forever. I can hardly bear to think about how much it might change the others'—especially if I choose wrong.

*Stop it*, I tell myself. *Use what you have.*

Hunches it is.

Rowley and Pratik are both too flashy, too noticeable, I think. If the extra is skilled enough to create false memories, it should be smart enough to want to blend in.

That leaves Brooke and Landilee.

I remember the moment when I realized it could be Brooke, the way she seemed unaccustomed to her own body, but that, too, felt too attention-getting. How could the extra be knowledgeable enough about humankind to become one in our minds but then do a poor job of disguising itself?

Landilee does creep me out, but that's probably just because she told that disturbing story, right? Surely the extra wouldn't make itself worthy of fear, either. Or maybe it would. Maybe it enjoys unnerving us. Or maybe it misjudged the true intent of campfire stories, which are not to scare, but to titillate.

Maybe she simply told her own story, unaware that we'd see her part in it as the boogieman. *I think, more than anything, he just wants to be let in. He just wants to belong.*

I look up, look around, looking for the thousandth time for something, anything to tell me what to think, what to do. It's overcast again and cold, but broad daylight. Everyone is chatting and moving along just fine. No one seems unnerved except me, Joey, and Bianca, but I know it, still. What I've felt from the beginning. Something's wrong.

I recognize the downshift in the trail. We're minutes from the stream. There are two, maybe three, more bends before we'll be able to see it through the trees.

Time's up.

My heart is racing.

I have Joey call a quick break and the three of us back off the trail until I'm sure we can't be heard. My 'crisis mode' calm seems to be wearing off. It's great when I can make an informed decision, but this...

My pulse is speeding, skin prickling with sweat in the cool air, my stomach a tight knot of squirming. I have to force myself not to pant.

"Who?" I ask, unable to talk more, to discuss.

Joey doesn't stall. "Gary."

I want to ask why, but I don't. That wasn't the deal. We both look at Bianca.

Reluctantly, she says, "Rowley. But I don't think that means we should leave him."

They look at me. I swallow once. "Landilee."

Bianca asks, "How do we vote if we each say someone different?"

I reply, "Does anyone have reasons they do or don't think it's one of those three?"

They both shake their heads.

I hedge, but come out with it. "Gary has a rash. I was thinking that rules him out."

"Yeah," Joey says, thinking. "Better than what I have. I'll change mine."

"Landilee or Rowley?"

He thinks for a long time, for which I'm grateful, but my nerves are so sharp I can practically feel them slicing up my insides. Finally, he says, "Landilee."

Bianca shoots him a look, but he doesn't meet her eyes. I don't know if she feels betrayed by him siding with me, or grateful that she won't have to carry any responsibility for the choice.

"Okay then. Bianca, I know you don't agree." I try to keep my tone gentle and not accusatory when I ask, "Have you come up with a different idea?"

Hunched over her arms where she clutches her stomach, she shakes her head.

I nod, resolved. I don't know if having decided makes me feel relieved or even more worried. Both, maybe. I'm on fire with nerves. "Y'all know the plan. Landilee is the last one to use the restroom."

None of us has to finish it:

And then we leave her behind.

# RULE #14: STAY FLEXIBLE TO ADAPT

I HOLD my breath as we cross back over the area of the green circle of grass, but it's no longer a vivid, unnatural green. The grass is sparse and drying, already mostly brown, and not noticeable. I can tell it's odd, but only because I know to look for it. I watch every face for a reaction to the area, but no one shows any signs of recognition or strange behavior besides me, Bianca, and Joey. We all cross the stream—much easier in the daylight—and pause at the other bank for a snack break.

At each of our campsites we designate a "restroom" area away from tents and bodies of water, as well as a specific tree branch at camp so we can hang the toilet paper; it helps protect privacy and prevent ourselves from being stumbled on while we're doing our business. If the TP is gone, you wait to go. Everyone just digs their own cathole. Normally we don't bother to choose a restroom during a simple snack break, but we also wouldn't stop for a snack break so close to the van at the end of the trip. Of course, none of the participants know that. We wrap it all in with everyone drying their feet and putting their hiking shoes back on. It's actually kind of nice. Maybe we'll do this from now on—or would, if I were ever going to run this trip again, which is feeling pretty unappealing at the moment. I can't imagine one hour from now, much less a year. Everything has become now, forever.

Joey and I choose a spot farther from the group than necessary. It's a little copse of trees with vivid red leaves. Privacy is good, but usually it's not beyond shouting distance. This time it might be. We'll need the terrain between us and Landilee.

After the fastest eaters have finished their bags of trail mix, I encourage them, one by one, to go use the restroom. I make a joke of it, using a parent tone to declare, "Everyone has to go before we leave the house."

Bianca's shooting me nervous looks as the remaining participants dwindle. We have to play it just right or it won't work. I don't want a show-down; I want a clean break. Fear of what this thing might be, and might be capable of, makes secrecy absolutely necessary. Not just for our peace of mind—for our survival. Landilee has to be the last one to go.

Finally, it's down to Meg, Landilee, and Diego. My voice sounding overly casual, I say, "Meg, you're up."

She shoots me a mildly startled look—not a big fan

of going outdoors. She's about to say no thanks. I can see it in her eyes, the refusal.

I add, "It'll be two and a half hours before we stop on the road."

Jo, most recently back, nudges her in the side with the roll of toilet paper, and Meg sighs. "Fine."

Down to two. Diego and Landilee. It's not surprising. Landilee has that mom-like self-sufficiency that makes her content to wait, and Diego is the solid. He hasn't left because he's been helping us out by gathering up the trash and stuff. Useful without being presumptuous. Just the ideal participant. There when we need him, inconspicuous when we don't.

Helpful. Quiet. Friendly. Likeable but not particularly memorable.

I freeze, my head down as I adjust something in my bag, not wanting anyone to see my face.

Could it be Diego?

No, I ruled him out. Why again? Oh, right. He's one of the ones with the rash.

Meg is coming back; I see her pink fleece through the trees, the blotch of the white toilet paper roll.

But Diego was the first one who got a rash.

He could've had it, given it to everyone else. That doesn't rule him out at all.

That could rule him very much in.

I like Diego. A lot, really. I'd have paid money to swap him for the vast majority of participants on any of my trips over the years. I don't want to leave him behind.

But if the extra is as smart as I think they are, they'd want to be likeable. They'd want to be wanted in the group.

I have moments to decide. Meg flounces toward us, holding the roll out for the next person. I'm supposed to direct that choice. It's supposed to be Diego, so Landilee goes last.

"I hate squatting," Meg faux-pouts, making a disgusted face. "That's one part of this trip I won't miss." She sees my face, which must look stricken, and quickly adds, "But the rest of it has been super cool though. Really."

I smile at her, but I'm sure it doesn't look real. Now. I have to choose now, or Meg will unknowingly choose for me.

I trust my gut.

"Landilee, you're up."

Bianca and Joey both gape at me, eyes huge with shock. It must seem like forsaking to them, but I have no time to consult with them. This should be my responsibility anyway, not theirs.

Luckily they're behind the older woman, so she doesn't see their shock. She barely glances at me. "I'm good."

Fuck.

Meg starts to shift toward Diego, but I say, "No, really. Everyone needs to go."

Landilee does look at me now, part annoyed and part surprised. "I don't need to go," she says with exasperation, like she's talking to a child.

But it's me who says the parent's line: "Just try. Humor me."

Rage flashes in her eyes, gleaming and quick. She's humiliated. I'm humiliated. I just couldn't come up with anything better so fast. She has to go. I don't break eye contact, turning it into a weird battle of wills. I can't back down now. I didn't mean to embarrass her, but this is too important. I can't have her realize she needs to go once Diego has left.

Meg is still standing with the toilet paper held out awkwardly.

"But Matt," Bianca says weakly, confused about why I've changed the decision. "Diego could..."

"Yep, next. Go ahead, Landilee. We're waiting on you."

All of the spit in my mouth has dried, leaving me cold and achy with panic, but I show nothing—only continue to look Landilee in the eyes, willing her to go.

She resists just long enough that I wonder if I've made a mistake. Has this gone from a prideful woman to an extra who knows it's about to be ditched?

But she reaches out to take the roll, never breaking my gaze until she turns to walk wordlessly up the trail. Her spine is stiff with outraged pride.

I stifle a sigh of relief.

Joey has come to stand beside Bianca, and I can tell he wants to put an arm around her. Neither of them can say anything. Not in front of Diego. They just have to trust that I know what I'm doing, that I have a reason for this.

Please let that trust be well-founded.

Diego, too, is watching me. It was a just strange enough interaction with Landilee to make that normal, justified. It wasn't a scene. No one else noticed anything; they all chat happily among themselves, paying us no mind. But Diego was right here. Meg watches us too, but it's Diego I'm suddenly aware of.

Does he know?

I work up enough spit to swallow, zipping my bag and standing. "Thanks for helping with the trash, man," I say to him. "You've been a big help on this trip. We really appreciate you." My voice is a hair too high.

"Hey, I'm happy to help."

I nod, unsure what else to say. I almost ask about his rash, but I don't want to bring it up. Not now.

Does he look suspicious, or am I projecting that?

Did I just send the extra away to make it safely back to the group?

Will Diego go? If he puts up enough of a fight, we won't be able to make him.

The van is less than five minutes away.

We've been standing in silence too long. Meg wanders awkwardly away from us, toward the larger group. She sits beside Jo, bumping softly into their side.

Finally, Landilee comes back. She very intentionally does not meet my gaze. I can't blame her.

She hands the roll to Bianca, who looks at me.

I try to tell her with my eyes that it's okay, then I

nod to Diego. "You're up. After you it's just us trip leaders and then we can hit the road."

He studies me for a few long seconds, but I've just reassured him we'll be here. If he's the extra, he might be suspicious. He might not fall for it.

I almost hope he doesn't.

I could be wrong. It could be any one of the other people. I can't know for sure. How can I live with myself if I'm wrong? And how will I know?

Is it him?

Diego takes the paper from Bianca and says, "Be back in a jiff."

I watch the group as he leaves. No one watches him go. When he's around the first bend, out of sight, I say quietly to Bianca and Joey, "Don't startle them, but get everyone moving. Quick. We don't know if he's on to us."

# RULE #15: LEAVE WHAT YOU FIND

THERE'S no time for Bianca and Joey to question me. There's no time.

Usually I always take the rear, but this time I need the group to move fast. I need them to match my pace.

With a bark of forced cheerfulness, I say, "Let's hit it, crew! I'm dying for a shower." Home. God, I want to be home.

My pace and sense of urgency works, and the group moves faster than normal down the trail. Joey, his voice cracking with what I can only imagine is panic, even sings a marching tune to get people going quicker.

I can't help looking back. I don't want anyone to notice that I keep looking back and realize we left someone behind, but I can't help looking. I don't see Diego. He's not catching up to us, which probably means he hasn't realized we're gone. When he does, he can run, and I can't get the group to run without alarming them.

Brooke is pink-faced and panting. I silently will her to hang on, keep trooping. We can't afford a stop right now.

I'm sweating too hard for how cold it is. My head is pounding. My heart will explode. I can't take it.

Finally, I catch a glimpse of the parking lot.

"Heeeeey, van!" I call, trying to get everyone pumped to get home so they'll move fast. "Packs in the trailer," I call, jogging ahead to unlock it and open all the doors.

I see the dog's paw prints in the dried mud, remember giving him the protein bar only to have him bite my hand. How hard it was to leave him behind. But as hard as it was, it'd been right. If I'd let the group bring him along, it could've been one of them who was bitten—and it could've been much worse. My priority has to be the good of the whole group. Wherever he is, I hope he's okay, but nothing good comes from bringing a wild thing home.

The trip leaders catch up with me and start gathering the bags of participants, tossing them into the trailer with uncharacteristic haste. A few people try to ask questions and Joey mows over them like a pro, happily ignoring time-consuming issues and ushering everyone inside.

Joey hops in after the last participant, pulling the sliding door shut after him. I leave Bianca to lock up the trailer, glancing at the trailhead. My heart is thundering. I can feel my face gone red. No one has mentioned Diego being gone.

I get into the driver's seat and turn to look.

The van seats are all full, save the passenger, which is for Bianca as she comes around the far side. There's that intense sensation of being able to smell everyone suddenly, now that we're inside the van. Sweat and smoke, dirty gear and body odor.

I wonder if everyone is sitting where they sat before. I don't remember and I can't find a casual way to ask. Would they even remember? Or would they remember whatever version the extra wants them to remember? Maybe the full seats are why no one mentions Diego. But maybe they don't notice for another reason. Maybe they don't notice because I chose right—because their memories of him, the extra, are already slipping away. I try to take comfort in that as Bianca comes to the open passenger door.

I gesture for her to get in, but she pauses, glancing toward the trailhead.

"Bianca," I say quietly, tone the type of calm that only comes on the surface of raging lower levels, "get in."

Her eyes are huge as she looks at me, terrified.

I feel that terror too, but we don't have time for it. "Please," I say, so quietly she probably only reads my lips.

I can see her pulse thumping under her jaw, making the vein below her ear twitch.

Mine feels like it's about to hop out and run away.

Finally, with harsh, jerky movements, she climbs into the seat and slams the door.

Out of nervous energy, I nearly shout, "Everyone buckle up!" I hear a chorus of seatbelts being drawn and snapped into place.

I look again toward the empty trailhead. No Diego. Yet.

But he has to be coming by now. He has to have found us gone and started on his way. Is he scared? Or angry? Or something I can't even begin to understand?

We need to go. Now.

Thank fuck that I've run so many goddamn trips that I can back up this beast with the trailer no problem. If one of my trip leaders were driving it could easily take ten minutes. I'm facing the exit of the parking lot in under one. I even hear someone from the back say, "Whoa."

A couple of participants have already started reminiscing about the trip, chatting about their favorite parts and funny things that happened, reshaping the experience into its final form in their minds.

No one mentions Diego. Does that mean he's the extra? That I chose right? Or is it just because he was a floater, along on his own, bouncing from person to group?

If the memories of him are fading for them, then why aren't they for me?

Will they?

My hands are shaking on the wheel. If I'm wrong, will he be okay out here? In the inclement weather and approaching off season, it could be days or even weeks before anyone else comes out to this area.

If he's the extra, that's good. I don't want anyone else bringing it home either.

But if I'm wrong...

If I'm wrong, I've not only done a horrible thing to Diego, but I've still put everyone else in danger. If I'm wrong, the extra is sitting right here with us, waiting to leave Diego behind. I look in the rearview mirror, but every face looks just as it should, friendly and familiar.

I glance in the side mirror—the rear view is blocked by the trailer behind us—and I think I catch the first glimpse of movement coming through the trees.

I don't wait to see. I don't wait to see who, or what, is coming toward us.

The van is full. No one has missed him.

I step on the gas and take us, abruptly, back onto the leaf-strewn road, the road that will carry ten warm bodies back home.

# ACKNOWLEDGMENTS

My first and biggest thanks for this one go to my husband Kyle, who was the inspiration for so much of it. Matt is no Kyle, but he was inspired by Kyle's former job role, and that endlessly generous source of information was vital to my capturing this particular trip. Not to mention that it was Kyle's telling of the river crossing portion of this story around a campfire that inspired me to combine this setting with my "extra" idea to begin with. Besides all of which, Kyle is my biggest supporter in every aspect of life, including writing, and I literally couldn't be doing what I do without him. I love you, Kyle.

Thanks to Alan Lastufka, who's an absolute pleasure to work with. I knew when I first saw your cover design that you "get it." Thanks for getting it, and for publishing me. You work unbelievably hard, and the quality reflects it. I am so proud to be a Shortwave author.

Thanks to my agent Alec Shane, who is a tireless champion of my writing and advocate for my career. You are a wonderful person to have in my corner, and I could not be more grateful for your faith, effort, and steadfast support over these years.

Thanks to Alex Langley for his constant friendship, encouragement, and feedback. Especially with this book, you have listened to me brainstorm and dream and worry and problem solve for more hours than you're paid for. You're my hype guy, my book bro, my literary wingman. So grateful for you.

Thanks also to Regina, Dan, and all of the writers from the Denton Writers' Critique Group who helped improve this 'short story that got out of hand' back when I first brought it in for feedback, and for generally pushing and teaching me as a writer. And to my writing partner Kelsey B. Toney, who has stood by me for years, who also offered critique on this one in the later stages. I wouldn't be the same without you.

There have been countless others who deserve acknowledgement too. To all of my friends for their love and support during this phase of my life. To my mom, brother, and family for their commiseration and celebration through all the years. And now my readers. Wow, my readers. Thank you for being here. I hope you take something home with you.

# ABOUT THE AUTHOR

**Annie Neugebauer** is a novelist, blogger, nationally award-winning poet, and two-time Bram Stoker Award®-nominated short story author. She writes horror, literary fiction, thriller, science fiction, fantasy, weird fiction, poetry, and anything sharp, dark, and beautiful that might linger in the mind. She has a penchant for high concept ideas and making readers question her mental health.

*The Extra* is her debut novella, with two shared-universe sequels forthcoming through Shortwave: *The Other* (2026) and *The Spare* (2027). Her debut short story collection, *You Have to Let Them Bleed*, is through Bad Hand Books.

Visit her at annieneugebauer.com, in most places under @AnnieNeugebauer, or frolicking through the abyss.

# A NOTE FROM SHORTWAVE PUBLISHING

Thank you for reading *The Extra*! If you enjoyed this book, please consider writing a review. Reviews help readers find more titles they may enjoy, and that helps us continue to publish titles like this.

For more Shortwave titles, visit us online. . .

**OUR WEBSITE**
shortwavepublishing.com

**SOCIAL MEDIA**
@ShortwaveBooks

**EMAIL US**
contact@shortwavepublishing.com